AISSA SAVED

Carfax
Edition

*With a new Prefatory
Essay by the Author*

THE NOVELS OF JOYCE CARY

JOYCE CARY

Aissa Saved

London
MICHAEL JOSEPH

First published in Great Britain by
MICHAEL JOSEPH LTD
52 Bedford Square
London W.C.1
1949
SECOND IMPRESSION DECEMBER 1950
FIRST PUBLISHED IN CARFAX EDITION 1952
REPRINTED MAY 1959
REPRINTED DECEMBER 1960
REPRINTED OCTOBER 1972

To

G.M.C.

*Printed in Great Britain by
Redwood Press Limited, Trowbridge, Wiltshire
and bound by James Burn at Esher, Surrey*

*a prefatory essay by the author specially
written for this edition*

★ ★ ★

THIS story began not with Aissa, but with Ali. He, under another name, was a chief's son from the Government school, sent to work in my office at Kaiama: I still remember his arrival, his extreme shyness, amounting almost to panic and (what I soon discovered) his efficiency and exact devotion to the job. He was a quite new kind of helper; he had quite different standards of conduct from anyone else in the administration.

I don't mean that none of the native officials was honest or capable. There is plenty of honesty in Africa as well as corruption. And quite often what we should call corruption is simply an accepted tradition. For instance, just after coming to the country, I was shocked to discover that a native justice took bribes. I reported him and was confident that my district officer would sack him.

My district officer did nothing of the sort. He went into the case and gave only a warning. He also told me that African justices were used to accepting presents from litigants—corruption did not arise unless the presents affected their judgments.

Of course the system is dangerous. But it cannot be abolished by decree. And when my own chief justice in Kaiama was accused by a disappointed highway robber of taking bribes, I blessed that early experience. For though bribery was proved from both sides, I remembered that the point was whether a right decision had been given. And I realized that it was just because he had given a fair decision that the chief justice had made powerful enemies. He was a good and conscientious man.

But Ali did not take bribes from anyone. Also he had a different standard of duty. He tried to do his job as well as it could be done.

Now the best of the others in that very primitive administration did their jobs carefully and well, but they had no notion of putting the job first. Their conception of duty was fulfilling a task, performing a function. And many other things came before the job.

Why I remember Ali so vividly is because he nearly gave his life for his ideal.

When I was pulled out of the army about 1917 after the Cameroons Campaign, and sent across the Niger to take over Borgu (it was then a piece of Kontagora Province) I was given some important looking maps, marked, War Office, 1910.

These maps turned out ludicrously bad; probably they had been made up from rough sketches sent in by officers during the first occupation about 1902. The same villages were entered in different places under different versions of their name. One planned a trek with such and such a halt, and when the column arrived found nothing but waterless bush. I had to make a new map.

But I had no skill or time for a proper triangulation, not even a plane table, only a compass with sights. As I rode along the tracks, I took compass bearings on some distant hill or tree, and ruled them down on paper. This gave me a series of overlapping triangles with the track as a common base.

But I had no wheel or pedometer to measure the track and no time to pace it out. So when I got to a camp about one hundred and thirty miles from the capital, I gave Ali the office clock (one of those tin American alarm clocks which were common in nurseries thirty years ago) and told him to walk along the road at his usual pace and write down the time of passing given points. He was also to note the time spent in meals.

I had tested Ali's walking speed at three and a half miles an hour. Ali with his usual very earnest expression went off with the clock and a note-book.

Three days later, while I was trying a case under a tree, one of the Emir's horsemen, covered with dust and sweat, came galloping up and shouted. 'From the Emir, Ali is dying—what instructions about the clock?'

And it turned out that Ali had walked a hundred and thirty miles without stopping except, very briefly, to eat. He hadn't understood that he could stop for the night.

Luckily he didn't die. He was only worn out and much upset by the notion that he had literally fallen down on his first big job. His record, in fact, *was* useless. The last thirty miles had taken him nearly as many hours.

He recovered quickly and did the work again. The map was accepted by Headquarters and I believe ended in a real Atlas. It may still be there. I hope so. I should be delighted to think that it was my first published work.

The story of Ali remained with me because it was exciting to see the effect of education on this rather shy, and not very clever boy. At the government school, the boys had their religious teaching from their own Mallams. They had their own wives and often their own houses and servants. Ali had learnt his ideas about duty simply by the way, in elementary arithmetic and history classes, on the football field, or in general talk with the European master.

I wanted to write about Ali because of this excitement. I was anxious to contrast Ali's standards and ideas with those about him. This, of course, involved questions of local ethics, local religion, the whole conflict of those ideas in a primitive community; and also the impact of new ideas from outside. And Aissa gradually became the heroine because she was more central to a deeper interest, that of religion. Ethics are important enough, goodness knows, but the fundamental question for everybody is what they live by; what is their faith. Why don't they cut their throats; why is the fakir happy on his nails; why does the millionaire shoot himself at the dude ranch.

All those in fact, who do not cut their throats and many who do, have some kind of faith; if only in a political theory, 'science', a mascot, or a column of mud roughly shaped like an erect penis.

The question is, how sound is the faith; how will it stand the big knock; how deep does it send its roots into reality.

The faith in juju stands badly, a few dry years, a very little 'contamination' from a government instructor destroys faith in the lingam.

And many who thought themselves sound Christians left the Church 'because of the war'. Their faith was in a God who apparently could stop wars if he would; who was, therefore, responsible for evil.

Some correspondents took the book for an attack on the Missions. It is not so. African missions have done good work in bringing to Africa a far better faith than any native construction. But it does try to show what can happen to the religious ideas of one region when they are imported into another.

I think, from experience, that some Christian missions do not realize the effect of telling African primitives that God is 'Almighty' or 'Omnipotent' and allowing them, uncorrected, to suppose that this means not 'the final power in the universe' but the 'one who can do all things.' So that they blame God for a sore throat, and thank him for a fine day or a good bargain.

I know that, in this respect, the Church is in the difficulty of all ancient institutions. It has inherited, like Parliament, articles of faith which were once taken in a literal sense but are now, by old believers, accepted as metaphors or symbols. And it can't change the form of expression without offending simple people.

But the trouble is that converts are obliged to accept the letter. They start, so to speak, several hundred years behind the old believers, in an age of absolutism and intolerance. There is quite a large danger that the religious wars of the fifteenth and sixteenth centuries in Europe should be imported to Africa. There was such a war in Uganda in the eighties of last century.

The book was my first, that is, the first completed. And as it is, it took three years to complete. The cause was partly inexperience, but chiefly, indecision. It raised a lot of questions in an acute form (such as why evil? and still more, why evil from good?) which I could not answer. I had waked up to the fact that all evil is not the result of an evil will; that the innocent may suffer the utmost misery; that there is such a thing as bad luck.

That is to say, I had realized the fundamental injustice of the world. It had 'come home' to me. And once a fact of that size 'comes home' it never goes away again. It is a permanent resident of the largest size and the most insistent voice. You can't 'get over' it.

And since my book arose from an experience of religion and meant to convey it, I had to know my own belief, exactly what I believed as distinct from what I thought I believed. It is hard to give an impression by means of words even when the object is clearly understood—to give a clear picture of one that is vaguely seen and continually melting away at the edges into a general landscape of other vague objects, is impossible.

Perhaps even then I might have been tempted to dodge some of the issues if I had not been so nervous a beginner in authorship. It seemed to me a very rash act to state or imply any truth which one was not prepared to explain or defend. Besides, I was convinced that my masters, Hardy, Conrad, James and the great Russians knew exactly what they meant.

I was like the man in Leacock (as near as I can recollect) who set out to build a henhouse, was troubled because he could not get the right nails; went into metallurgy and died forty years later, still without a henhouse, as a first year student in chrystallography.

I did actually finish my henhouse, but only with much trouble. For when I had found answers to my own problems, I tried to put them in the book. Like anyone who has broken, with difficulty, out of a confused foggy disintegrated state of feeling and thought into moderately clear going, I wanted to tell everyone how to find the road. I did not realize that everyone has his own fog and therefore, needs a special map; that most of those who wanted a way out had found it for themselves, and that the rest would rather stay where they were; that is, different people needed different kinds of faith; 'true' for them.

So being eager, not only to understand for myself but to show what was understood, I invented new occasions and even some new characters whose function was to illustrate or even to discuss, aspects of the question.

It might be worth saying here that such talk would not have been out of place in a book about West Africa. I have sat up half the night, many times, beside camp fires, discussing 'providence, foreknowledge, will and fate' with other bush officers.

The bush, the night sky, the sense of isolation in large spaces equally indifferent and alien, whether as tropical blackness crowded with too-bright stars or pitch dark forest filled with all the mysterious comings and goings of African nighttime, rustlings, creakings, murmurs, sighs, drumming, the cough of some beast, the squeal of some bird; not to speak of the death rate, in those days, among white officers (three died of yellow jack in one year) seemed to encourage such speculations.

I had a good excuse for bringing 'Russian colloquy' into my book, and I brought a good deal into the early versions, producing an immense and complex work.

Luckily the same diffidence as author, which made me anxious to know what I was doing before I ventured on a serious book, filled me with alarm at the result. I found it clumsy and dull. As my own critic I rejected it and I fancied that publishers would do the same. And so I cut out the religious philosophising (chiefly between Bradgate and the Carrs) and rewrote the book several times in forms of increasing simplicity. That is why it took three years to finish.

J. C.

1 Shibi Rest Camp on the Niger was built by Bradgate, then assistant resident, about 1912. He wanted to make his station there, but the doctors refused to pass the site on account of the swamps close behind which fill it with mosquitoes.

Afterwards the Winkworth Memorial Mission obtained leave to use the buildings and added to them a chapel and hospital.

Bradgate, like other sportsmen, had an eye for views. The Niger is half a mile wide at Shibi and the high mud bank which he chose for his site is a peninsula three parts detached from the low shore behind. It is shaped like a boat, with a round stern and a long sharp bow pointing into the stream, which rushes past on the outside like the waves sheared away by a steamer. So that if you turn your back on Shibi the boat appears to be at sea with miles of open water in front and behind, and the coast of Yanrin a long way off, a mere line of grey bush and pale brown village dividing the huge sheet of crinkled, glittering water below and the radiance of half a universe overhead. On a hot day Yanrin seems to float on the current, rocks up and down, wriggles like a sea-serpent and then changes into a streak of smoke or wind.

Visitors to Shibi used to admire these fine views and listen with delight to the sound of lapping water all round them, which made it a pleasure even to lie awake at night, but the missioners, Mr. and Mrs. Carr, did not seem to be convinced. Even to Bradgate, who came expecting some praise for his favourite rest camp, and whom they entertained with the honours due to the District Officer of Yanrin, they scarcely pretended enthusiasm. They answered him politely that it was very pretty, that the sunsets were nice, but their expressions

13

showed that they had more important things to do than admire views. Bradgate, in fact, was made to feel a trifle frivolous. The very children regarded him with solemn, reproachful eyes. Mrs. Carr's maid, Aissa, a half-bred Fulani girl with big soft eyes and a fine golden skin very attractive to any man, whom he met trotting across the yard with a fat baby nodding on her back and a basket of wet clothes on her head, turned aside from him as if from a contamination.

'I think you come from Kolu, in my country,' he said to her, with that friendly smile which he used to reassure the timid native. But the girl did not even glance at him. 'Pardon,' she murmured, and flew by with her severe nun-like expression. Bradgate affected great amusement, and as he strolled about, he smiled jovially upon everything and everybody, as if to say, 'Bless you, my children, play away, be happy.'

2 This was at eight o'clock when everybody came into the open and assumed his public demeanour, when the builders laying out their new bricks to dry in the sun (and the builders were not even converts) wore the air of statesmen, and the scavenger carrying his buckets to the latrine frowned like a pontif (or like Carr) and stared before him with the rapt gaze of a saint or a Mrs. Carr.

The mission rose at six but eight was the time for a change of duty. At that time the Carrs went to breakfast, where they discussed anxiously the plans of the day, food, mission clothes, the sick, the services, interviewing suppliants and hearing reports at the same time; the out-patients, their wounds dressed before breakfast, were crawling back to Shibi village, and the women, having cleaned their compound, came to sewing class in the chapel.

This chapel, built of mud, with large square holes for door

and windows, was the joy and pride of the Carrs. It had even a tower, and in the tower a bell made out of a shell case. The broad, thatched roof came almost to the ground on each side, where it was supported on short crooked posts.

These two shady corridors along each side of the chapel served as cloisters and lecture rooms. The sewing class under old Sara, leader of the women, met on the north side where already, in the slanting rays of the sun which crossed half the floor, they were grouped like a large show-bank of blue, white, and yellow blooms.

Within the chapel itself the chief pupil teacher was instructing the choir in English. His high voice could be heard incessantly lecturing and imploring, and in its notes could be detected the intonations of both the Carrs. One would have said that it was Mrs. Carr, a Mrs. Carr rather drunk and hysterical if that were possible, who repeated, 'Jesus,' 'God,' 'Lord have mercy upon me,' all the words of devotion; and Carr's voice which said briskly and with impatience: 'No, no, dat's no good. *Can't* you listen?'

The boy managed even to look like Carr, in spite of his unwholesome, tobacco-coloured face, his pug nose, his one eye closed up by a blow and the other large and rolling, suffused with blood, when he thrust his long thin neck round the corner of the chapel door and shouted angrily at the Bible class in the south aisle: 'Be quiet, dere. What you tink you doing? You tink dis a beer house?'

He spoke with authority, and the sounds of a free fight coming from the Bible class stopped abruptly and did not begin again for half a minute. Ojo was an acknowledged leader in the mission on account of his intelligence and religious convictions. Only a week before he had interrupted a pagan dance in Shibi, and received a beating which had covered him with bruises and nearly knocked out one eye. He would have been killed if a wandering policeman from Berua had not happened to come by and driven off the angry women in the name of the Emir.

He was a Yoruba boy, once a trader's servant, who had spent most of his life in prisons and hospitals. His ambitions had always urged him to take short cuts to glory and honour. He was too impatient to save and so he stole and swindled. His passions were not mixed with calculation, and so he had seized the first woman available and the nearest drink. The Carrs, who knew his kind very well, a kind turned out every year in large quantities by the new civilization of the coast, had rescued him from a native gaol where he was dying of misery and two or three diseases, including syphilis. They were confident of turning to good a creature so quick witted and emotional, and they had not been wrong. Ojo was now the most faithful and devoted of their pupils. His love for Jesus, who had saved him from his wretchedness, had proved sincere and lasting.

Ojo was shocked by the irreverent conduct of the Bible class in the precincts of the chapel, but such as Nagulo, a highway robber and murderer, Salé, an old soldier from the Cameroons, Frederick, the small boy, from a mission school on the coast, Shangoedi, an epileptic woman from Kolu and Aditutu, lately a drunken midwife, were not easily overawed. Nagulo, a man uglier than a frog and more powerful than an orang-outang, both of which he resembled, cut off in the middle of a yell, with his fists in the air and the foam on his lips, remained in the same position, with an expression of surprise, for about twenty seconds, and then uttered a loud laugh. He was not laughing at Ojo but at his own annoyance. He dropped his hands with a loud slap on his knees, spat into the sunlight, blew his nose with his fingers and bawled: 'Come, woman, I desire you. It's time for the play.' This was a quotation from a pagan song used at the festivals of Oke in Yanrin, and it was received with shouts from the men and giggles from the women.

The girl Aissa threw her cloth over her face and gave a loud scream, as if she had been pricked. Her whole body quivered with excited laughter.

But Frederick, an Ejaw boy of twelve, as beautiful and fragile as a young Jewess, cursed them both in three languages: 'You fool man, Nagulo; you bad woman, you slut, Aissa, you go Kolu den dey kill you dere, dey chop you.'

Immediately Nagulo threw himself at him, Salé, who agreed with Frederick, caught hold of Nagulo, Aissa beat Salé, and Salé abused Aditutu. Screams and roars were heard, like the battle cries of lions and stallions. The discussion of this point was always animated because the Carrs themselves did not agree upon it. Was the next mission meeting to be at Kolu or a village nearby called Sabongari? Should the women be allowed to go or only men?

Both towns were on the Yanrin coast, long closed to missionaries after the murder of a Belgian priest there in 1909. Kolu was the pagan capital where just at that time all the tribes in Yanrin were gathering for a rain-making feast; Sabongari, a small trading settlement where Christians were welcomed.

The rival parties were quite as angry and obstinate as those of a Sunday School at home debating the place and time of the annual treat. No one was surprised to see Aissa, star of the confirmation class, spit in Frederick's face, or to hear old Kalé, the leper, revered by everyone for his humility and gentleness, use language worse even than Aditutu's. But a single squeak of warning from the little girl, whose duty it was to look out from the door, procured instant silence and a wild scramble for places. Huge men like Nagulo and Salé jostled for seats with children wearing their hair in a single topknot, and having won the contest sat grinning with relief and satisfaction, like schoolboys who have got out of a scrape.

The Carrs had come out from breakfast and now stood in

the full glare of the sunlight and in view from all three classes. The singing in the chapel had stopped and the sewing girls were poking their heads out of their verandah. Thirty pairs of eyes accustomed from their first years to study the demeanour of autocrats gazed intently at the white people to divine their mood and what was to be expected of it. Were they in a good temper? Were they brisk or tired? Were they allies to be feared as one or enemies to be inflamed against each other?

Carr was smiling at his wife in a peculiar manner, which caused Aissa to say at once with confidence: 'They've been fighting again.' The smile told them all that the master was angry with the mistress but desired to hide his anger from them. He held his bicycle in one hand, slightly raised his helmet with the other and made some remark.

The woman looked at him for a moment but did not answer. It was easily seen that she wanted to make some answer but could not think of one.

The little man with a skip and a hop mounted his bicycle and rode away. Every movement of his sharp knees, jumping violently up and down, and his narrow tight behind wriggling on the saddle, expressed furious irritation.

Mrs. Carr dragged herself wearily across the hot clay. Her thin face, of a greenish tint in the shadow of her wide-brimmed hat, glistened with sweat, which made bright drops reflecting the yellow earth beneath her nose and small round chin. Her eyes, pale like the water of the river, gazed into the air with a mournful expression which at once communicated itself to the watchers, so that all eyes, black and brown, the little blood-shot pig's eyes of Nagulo and the huge eye, like a nervous hare's, of Ojo, rounded themselves in unconscious sympathy or imitation.

But suddenly catching sight of Ojo's head projecting from the chapel door she recovered herself, made a little movement of her shoulders like one adjusting a weight, her glance became familiar, she moved with a brisker step, smiled, and after a moment's thought made the necessary greetings.

'Good morning, Ojo, why haven't I seen you before. You know you should have come to get your eye dressed.'

Ojo, too, was brisk and businesslike. His eye had been dressed by Aissa, he made light of it with a careless gesture.

'Some people here ask me we go to Kolu, Ma, I say no know.' Hilda smiled and remarked that his class was waiting for him.

Ojo, thus gently snubbed, vanished into the twilight of the chapel. Old Kalé in the verandah ran to fetch his mistress a chair. 'Is it Sabongari?' he murmured in Hausa.

'I don't know, Kalé,' and then to show them that she did not want any more questions, she quickly asked Nagulo to repeat the last lesson.

Nagulo, frowning, half shutting his eyes, his narrow brow wrinkled with the effort, began to tell, in broken phrases, the story of the gadarene swine. 'And de—dere was some pigs dere, ma. Close to dat place, dere was some pigs. And when de evil spirits——' He stopped, breathing hard. A little pop-eyed girl beside him, leaping on her heels in her impatience, her face shining with the pride of knowledge, waved her arms in the air, wrung her hands in impatience; old Kalé too smiled as if to say: 'That's easy, just ask me.' Other forms jerked, other arms waved in the second row, and ejaculations expressive of amusement and scorn rose like a gust.

But Mrs. Carr stilled them with a glance, and then turning again her sympathetic look upon Nagulo, prompted him in her most encouraging voice: 'Evil spirits, Nagulo. Were there many then?'

'A tousand, ma—tousands, yes, and Jesus he say, you go into dem pigs now, you evil spirits.'

The stupid old blackguard was sweating in his haste and anxiety to avoid the shame of her reproach.

19

Visitors like Bradgate were always astonished to see such as Nagulo in the class and to hear them tell in English the stories of Noah, Solomon, the feeding of the multitudes, the marriage at Cana. But to the Carrs it was the visitor's astonishment which was surprising. Mrs. Carr would say indignantly to some political officer of twenty years' standing: 'You think these people are stupid because you don't teach them anything. They are just as clever as people at home, and much more anxious to learn.'

But the Carrs were more successful at Shibi than any of their predecessors. The reason was that they were liked. Their lessons were easily learned and firmly believed by those who felt their sincerity, unselfishness and sympathy, goodness of a kind recognized by every tribe and family in the world, even by dogs, horses and cats.

3 Mrs. Carr had always had a feeling, as she said, that the mission party ought to go to Kolu direct, in order to strike a powerful blow at paganism in one of its most important centres, but at that time it appeared to Carr stupid and even wicked to risk trouble with the government and perhaps the total prohibition of Christian work in Yanrin by provoking the Kolua during a feast. He pointed out also that Bradgate's unexpected visit made it impossible to hide their plans from him, and that he was very likely to forbid any landing in Yanrin, especially at Kolu.

But Bradgate, suddenly pleading great urgency of business, went away before lunch and at the last minute Carr changed his mind about Kolu. It happened in this way. He had arranged to be called at four in the morning which was the time already fixed for the expedition to Sabongari, but was allowed to sleep till a quarter past that hour, when an excited small boy and an old man from the hospital with guinea worm in both legs came into the house shouting that the whole mission had gone to the feast.

It was that Ojo, the small boy explained with great indignation; and that Aissa. 'She's always wanted to get off to Kolu ever since somebody told her that her blackguard man Gajere was out of gaol again. She's mad about him, the slut. And then the women went after Aissa. Where she goes they all want to go.'

'All gone,' shouted the old man, who was obviously thrown into great alarm by an event so unusual and mysterious. 'I saw them on the Shibi road, Ma, too, I saw her running after them.' His voice rose to a squeak and his eyebrows were arched into the middle of his forehead.

In fact Mrs. Carr's bed was empty, and her clothes gone.

Carr seized the nearest lantern and ran off to Shibi village as fast as he could go, taking a short cut through the swamps, which were fortunately harder than usual after a prolonged dry season. But he was in such a hurry and fright that he lost his way, tumbled into holes and thickets, and did not see the smoke and flames blowing from the lantern which peppered him from head to foot with large black smuts. Finally it went out and left him struggling in a thicket. He did not reach Shibi by the short cut, a mile long, in half an hour.

He found the whole population awake. Family parties were crowded on the bank which was lighted by several great bon-fires and dozens of grass torches, whose sudden flashes showed other groups farther off and the interested, startled faces of children staring out of doors and window holes.

All these townspeople standing close together for warmth were still and silent. The mission party was making all the noise which Carr had heard for the last half hour. Splashing about in the water, arguing, pushing, all shouting advice, instructions, with shrieks of laughter and indignation, they seemed like a crowd of excited children going on a school treat.

21

All wore their best clothes. Ojo, marked out from some distance by his damaged eye, which protruded like a burst fig, was standing up to his thighs in the water in his white uniform coat. On his head was balanced his folded trousers and his hymn book, in one hand he held a lantern and in the other a pair of patent leather shoes glittering as brightly in the yellow and red reflections of the fires as the black waves beneath. He was yelling something of which not one syllable could be distinguished in the hubbub.

Carr shouted to him to come to land. 'Come in at once, Ojo. What are you doing there?'

Ojo, chancing suddenly to catch his master's eye, looked very much alarmed, then turned and pushed his way through the water to a large dug-out. He was at once lifted in and the boat was paddled quickly away.

At the same moment a long flame rising from one of the bonfires showed other boats farther off, and farthest of all one full of women, suddenly revealed in the middle of the darkness like a fine ivory carving on a shelf of black glass. The women crowding it from end to end, surprised by the same glare, turned their faces towards the shore and laughed. Carr recognized Aissa laughing as usual with her whole body, her shoulders up to her ears and her hands clasped in ecstasy. Then she threw her cloth over her face.

Carr seeing that this boatful of young girls could not be allowed to go to Kolu alone, and that if it passed beyond recall he and the rest must follow, rushed into the water towards it, beckoning with his arm and shouting at the top of his voice.

But the flame went out, the boat vanished and no one paid any attention to the angry white man forcing his way to and fro in the water; probably no one noticed him.

He himself, as he turned furiously right and left, could not recognize known features among the huge grinning mouths and rolling eyes that darted by him in the broken light, and in fact they were not known to him. They were not those demure or responsible European expressions to which he was accustomed in the mission, but holiday faces that had never shown themselves there.

Suddenly he caught sight of his wife standing on the bank near one of the fires. She was hot and breathless, her eyes glittering with fatigue and excitement. In one hand she carried a furled sun umbrella with which she appeared to be threatening the headman of boats, a big Nupe, who bent forward towards the top of her head with a look of the most humble alarm.

He ran to her, but before he could utter a word she saw him and began to pour out explanations so rapidly that it was impossible to pick the weakest. Ojo had had a call to go to Kolu—the spirit had spoken to him in the men's club room, so he said, but of course it was difficult to say exactly what he meant by that—and Aissa had volunteered to go with him—and all the women ran after Aissa to make sure of not being left out. She had been waked by the noise.

'I ran down as fast as I could, but of course I was much too late to catch them. Luckily there are plenty of boats, though of course Sarkin Kogi tried to make me believe that they're all let out for to-morrow; what he's really afraid of is that there'll be trouble on the other side, and the Kolua may try to keep them, but I told him that we'd report him to the resident and he soon changed his tune. He's got his very best boat for us, I was determined you shouldn't get wet again, dear, they're just putting it straight now.'

She pointed at a long heavy dugout at the bottom of the bank, from which two men were hastily bailing dirty water and fish offal. A heap of clean mats had been piled up amidships as a seat for the passengers.

'Ojo had a call!' said Carr dryly.

'Yes, dear.' She looked at him with a glance at once timid and defiant. He knew that she believed in such calls.

'You mean that he was bored with teaching stupid pagans in Shibi and wanted a little excitement and glory.'

'Shall we go, darling? I'm so afraid that Aissa will get there first and do something reckless.'

'I suppose there's nothing else for us to do.'

He handed her down the bank and the crew, eager to start, since the rest of the fleet had already disappeared round the first headland upstream, at once pushed off. Their loud grunts and the quick splashing of their poles, the little eager cries of the headman showed their delight in following the others, in not being alone.

'Ojo seems to me a bit of a degenerate,' said Carr. 'He enjoys working himself up about things. And Aissa is nothing but a common or garden trollop.'

This was too much for Mrs. Carr even in her tactfulness; she answered indignantly that Aissa was a very good girl.

'She has one of the most affectionate natures I've ever known in a native girl, truly affectionate, I mean, and she's sincere in her religion too. I've seen her going into the chapel by herself time and again. I really believe she goes every day; she never goes past without saying a prayer.'

'Yes, I've noticed that, there's no doubt she's been up to something for some time. As for the affectionate nature, she's apparently run off to Kolu to find a man for herself—there's no doubt at least about her appetites.'

After this for a long time they were silent. Many quarrels had taught them the futility of argument. Hilda told herself that her husband did not mean what he said; he was tired, ill, over-burdened with work and responsibility. She easily excused him for a passing meanness of spirit.

Carr, for his part, reflected bitterly that his six months' work of preparation and diplomacy with Bradgate was in jeopardy because his wife had no more judgment or common sense than uneducated savages like Ojo and Aissa. She did not even want them. Why had he married? How right the Catholics were to save their priests from that folly. Your religious woman was worse even than the rest because she had an excuse for not shinking. They were all anti-rational in spirit, gamblers, sentualists, seeking every chance to escape from the trouble of planning and deciding, into some excitement or other. For such as Hilda, lame, sick, tortured by worry and anxiety, an adventure like the Kolu expedition offered itself like an escape. She flew to it like a clerk to war or a ruined man to drink. But it was no good explaining this to her because she had no brain to understand it and a complete answer to all criticism. What she felt to be right was God's will.

He sighed and wrapped his wet legs in a mat. He would certainly have a return of his rheumatism and all for nothing.

It was queer that on this night alone in months he should have slept less badly than his wife. And why had the lamp failed him? It had plenty of oil in it. It had never played tricks before. But why should he be surprised, luck was always against him—if one could call an enemy so persistent and malignant, luck.

Once again, as on other sleepless nights, less miserable and anxious than this one, Carr felt his enemy as a personal force, as the Devil himself, penetrating all existence, as manifold and plastic as life itself, but much more cunning. He could feel him in the immense darkness which surrounded him, like a watchful breathing soul.

How could you defeat a power which was capable of using such as Ojo and Hilda for his own ends? How could you fight against ambition taking itself for public spirit and egotism pretending to be dependence on God's will. Or even come to grips

25

with greed, lust and selfishness, which could change their very being and appear as industry, love, chastity, and thoughtfulness. And what could you do against the fools? It was not wicked to be foolish, but it was the fools did most of the Devil's dirtiest work. And when would fools cease to be? The fight was obviously hopeless and probably useless. Was he not the biggest fool of the whole party to throw away his health and peace of mind and his best years on such a struggle?

4 At dawn, as Carr had feared, the whole fleet was discovered still in midstream and scattered over a mile of water. The women's boat, still far ahead, was nearest to the shore current which was already beginning to carry it faster than the rest towards Kolu Bay. The men were shouting at them. Carr also waved and shouted but they pretended not to hear. Then one by one, the other boats, lifted on the strong eddy, began to fly after them as if sliding down a hill.

Kolu town is in two parts, divided by a market place larger than both of them together. The new town, on the waterside, inhabited by Hausas, Nupes, Yorubas, the mixed population of a harbour, has many flat-topped houses and even tin roofs, which give it a ramshackle modern air. The old pagan town on the other side of the market place resembles a thick mass of bee skeps clustered tightly together on a long row of small hills. The pointed tops of its huts and corn bins make an irregular fringe against the sky in every direction.

As the sun rose its first rays caught the points of these roofs, so that they looked like ripe corn stooks in a high, wide field. All below its level, the market place and the new town, was submerged in a brown shadow. But as the boats drifted together into slack water, a hundred yards from the shore, it could be seen that this pond of shadow was crowded with people as thick as ants over the nest, moving in and out among the houses and intermingling on the open ground, not in confusion but in lines and figures which continually broke, reformed, crossed and avoided one another as if in a slow dance.

The women and boys in the first boats, who had been laughing and chattering all night, teasing and shouting jokes from boat to boat, now suddenly became silent. All gazed at the town, now seen extended round its wide bay through a half part of the horizon, with surprise and awe, as if they had never seen it before. One of the girls said in a frightened voice: 'Look, look, it's full of pagans.'

'Those are the ones that eat people,' said another, and every face with rounded eyes, hanging lips, showed alarm and wonder as if asking: 'Why did I come here?'

'Master was calling to us, we ought to go back,' a boy's voice declared, and immediately a furious dispute broke out among the women, between Aissa and Shangoedi, who wanted to go on, and the rest, who wanted to go back.

'Here he is now,' said the boy with great relish. 'He'll give you trouble, you girls.'

This at once put an end to the angry shrieks of the women, who turned and looked anxiously towards Carr, whose big dugout, paddled at its full speed, came darting down on them through showers of glistening drops. Carr himself was standing up amidships and seemed already to threaten them with his angry expression and waving arms.

The women, suddenly finding their presence of mind, shouted to their headman to go back. 'Hi, you there, get to work. Quick, you old fool.' Some tried to take up the paddles themselves. But at this moment of panic Ojo's voice, rising with its usual fervent tenor note from the middle boat, sang the first words of a hymn.

At once it was taken up by the faithful ones about him, by

old Kalé, Nagulo and Makoto. Aissa and her friends, the three or four town-bred girls who always went about with her, came in as one shrill defiant yell in the treble, like a battle cry.

They sang even louder when Carr's boat at last floated among them, but as they stared anxiously at him they saw to their surprise that he, too, and Mrs. Carr, were singing with them:

'Yet He found me, I beheld Him
Bleeding on the accursed tree,
Heard Him pray forgive them, Father.'

The sight of the white woman's face, radiant with joy and triumphant courage, and of their master's enthusiasm as he beat time vigorously with her hand tightly grasped in his, removed all their doubts. Every voice joined in, and loud cries urged the paddlers to go on.

But in fact it was only at the last moment that Carr had changed his intention of putting a stop to the expedition, and with a suddenness which appeared both to Hilda and himself as providential and even miraculous. It was the hymn, always a favourite at the mission, which converted him. It had always strongly affected him, but now its words of devotion, sounding with unusual beauty over the water in the clear bright air of the morning, thrilling with the girls' voices and the ecstasy of his wife's spirit beside him, came upon him with overwhelming force. He felt again that powerful wave of emotion which he had known years before and not since, and recognized as the call to his ministry and its justification. His eyes filled with tears, his pride revolted from the mean anxieties of the night. He saw, as in a flash of lightning, the way out of the dark confusion in which he had been struggling so long and desperately, with problems never to be finally solved and difficulties renewed every day, the way of faith which he had been pointing out to savages daily for ten years and wandered from himself.

'Trust God,' he had told them; 'take no thought for the morrow,' while he had been trusting everything and everybody

28

but God, his own intelligence and forethought most of all. And it had brought him, as he could have foretold for anybody else, into the pit of the last night, to cowardice and despair of which the lowest pagan might have been ashamed. He had called his wife a fool, but he was the fool, the typical fool of the world, full of conceit and cocksureness. Like all the blind materialists, the grabbers, the hogs and donkeys of a society which he had despised and rejected, he had despised in her just that which made her better than he—her humility, her faith.

He pressed her fingers and she, turning without ceasing to sing, looked at him steadily and smiled. It was obvious that she had understood him at once and was not in the least surprised by his change of heart. There was no triumph in her affectionate delight, she was sharing his elation.

With what gratitude for her love and sympathy, for all God's goodness and the power of His Spirit, he joined with her in the crowning verse:

> 'Lord Thy love at last has conquered,
> Grant me now my soul's desire,
> None of self and all of Thee.'

How simple those words, containing all the wisdom of Jesus, and the whole creed of His ancient church, how powerful to cleanse and heal the soul. None of self and all of thee—there was no middle way. All his hours of anxious planning, his nights of apprehension made unnecessary. Brain and nerves and courage enjoyed release like a resurrection. He did not care for anything or anybody.

A line of watchers had begun to form on the shore. In a few moments it extended half a mile along the water's edge as still and solid as an oak paling.

5 Kolu was crowded for the feast on account of a religious revival. The drought and bad prices of 1921 which followed the boom years of the war hurt the pagans, who were farmers, much more than the Mahomedan tradesmen; the villages were full of half-starved people whose stores were nearly finished, whose children were hungry and who expected to die in the most miserable fashion if the rains did not fall and the crops did not grow. They were frightened, and they were determined to find out why so many troubles, bad crops, bad prices, late rains, one after another, had fallen upon them.

The Kolua are an intelligent, brave people. They know that every effect has a cause, and they are not prepared to call any cause hopeless of improvement.

At first no one could find out any reason for the slump and the bad crops. Some blamed the Hausa corn traders, beat them and threw them in the river; others declared that the Mahomedans had put a spell on the yam fields.

The judge told everybody that the slump was due to the end of the war and the bad crops to the weather, which could not be helped; and the Emir said that famine, if it came, was God's will and nothing could be done to avert it. But these statements were obviously absurd. As a pagan chief said: 'This white man does not know anything about our country and the Emir is tired and does not care about anything. These rulers want to keep us quiet, to send us to sleep. But we shall not be sent to sleep. We shall look for this person who has cursed our crops and stopped the rain; until we die we shall look, for we are not Mahomedans or Christians who lie down in trouble like a dog waiting to be whipped.'

It was at this time when the rains of the new season also were overdue that Owule, an old priest who looked after the sacred grove and juju house at a place called Ketemfe, began to go through the villages telling the people that their troubles were due to the displeasure of Oke.

Oke is the Kolua goddess of mountains and fertility, and every logical person in Yanrin saw at once that if Oke was indeed offended the bad rains, the bad harvest, the drought were easily explained. But why was she offended? Had they not besought her for good crops, and given her double the usual sacrifices?

'Yes,' said Owule, 'but nevertheless she is offended. This is proved by the absence of good yams and early rains. Therefore your sacrifices are not good enough and you had better repent before her.'

Owule had not only good arguments but all the influence which derives from sincerity and age. Moreover, when the old man who was almost blind and crippled by rheumatism had hobbled as far as Kolu, his denunciations and appeals were confirmed by Oke herself.

She showed herself to an epileptic girl at twilight on the main Yanrin road and bitterly complained of the people's bad conduct towards her. Within the next week she was seen by dozens of people all over Yanrin, sometimes in two or three places at once, in woods, in houses, in the beer shops, in the crowded market place, and always she reproached them, frequently in the same words, for their cold hearts, their selfishness, their meanness and their doubt.

She came to her own priestess, Moshalo, at night, and placing one hand across her breasts, the other between her thighs, she said that no rain would fall until the people gave her a virgin girl or boy.

This request alarmed all the chiefs and headmen, especially the Emir and the Mahomedans on the council, who pointed out that if the district officer or the new missionary at Shibi came to hear of a sacrifice they would make trouble.

31

'May they be cursed for oppressors and strangers, but at present they are strong and their whims have to be regarded.'

But the people answered, 'Better to be fined or imprisoned than see our children starved.' And what lent even greater force to their demand and made it dangerous was their knowledge that they themselves would not be fined or imprisoned, they were too poor and numerous. The white man's punishment would fall on some priest or village head.

The Emir's council was in session for five hours on the day before the Oke feast, but since of its eight members four were Mahomedans and four pagans it did not reach a decision. This council was intended to be representative and so far demo-cratic. The arrangement had certainly produced more discussion than any former one.

6 Many country people travelled all night to reach Kolu for the feast day. From five o'clock they walked the streets. The tired women, dusty from their long journeys, opened their cloths towards the men and chanted in bored voices the ritual song beginning, 'In the middle of my body I have a womb.'

The men gave the conventional answer and passed. Most of them had the same anxious and preoccupied looks as the women. They drew into groups, looking at the sky and mutter-ing among themselves. 'There's no chance. It's these Yorubas and white men. No wonder Oke is angry.'

'Well, this is the end of us. I'm surprised it hasn't come before.'

Some of the young men, led by a certain Ajala, a devoted follower of the old religion, reproached the Christians with everything, and several people in the pagan town who had been to Shibi mission for medicine or advice were abused. One old man, a greatly respected citizen whose family had inhabited the same site for many generations was knocked down and beaten because two of his sons, Gani and Makoto, both ne'er-do-wells and drunkards, had become Christians. This old father, whose name was Makunde, would have been burnt out of his house if his wife Marimi had not run out with her children and began to dance in the road and to sing the ritual song in its most elaborate form. She, like other worthy residents, quiet people, had performed her religious duties early in the day, and did not care to repeat them as a spectacle for the crowd. But she saved her house and husband by her wild howls and vigorous gestures which made the young men laugh and drew them away from the place.

She hobbled down the road performing the steps and jerks with paralytic movements like those of a wooden toy; and after her a grand-daughter, about ten years old, who had put on a cloth for the first time that day, in order to carry out the motions of the dance, trotted after her, opening the cloth towards the walls of the houses and the empty road, curtseying right and left and murmuring, 'If you have the wherewithall of a man, come to me, it is your duty.'

This child, whose name was Tanawe, pleased the bystanders by her shyness almost as much as old Marimi amused them. Shyness in children is an admired quality in Kolu because it speaks of innocence and gentleness which excite affection and the protective instinct in everybody of the same kind, that is, man for man, or dog for dog. Kolu children of old-fashioned families like Makunde's were remarkable for their gravity and decorum; because, though they were much loved, they were strictly brought up and made to behave themselves as far as possible like grown-ups. Tanawe like the rest found this treatment very reasonable because she wanted to be as grown-up as possible. Therefore in spite of her shyness she performed the Oke dance with care and carried herself with dignity. She

33

felt her responsibility. This was not a game, it was something important.

Behind Tanawe a little boy of eight called Numi, naked and with a protruding stomach, walked with a scared face and murmured inaudibly: 'I am a man.' He was Tanawe's cousin, the son of a woman called Ishe who had just turned aside from the party to answer some remark of an enemy; but Numi followed Tanawe and kept close to her because he trusted her more than his mother. He considered her wiser than his parents whom he had already perceived to be no good. His father was a fool; his mother was poor and unlucky, always quarrelling. Bad luck and poverty had made her irritable, and when she quarrelled, as happened every day, she showed such anger and ill will that many people called her a witch. Numi seeing her feared and despised by respectable people had no confidence in her. But he had no confidence in anybody, and so while he sang, 'I am a man,' he looked frightened and searched for Tanawe's hand.

Yemaja, another of the cousins, was laughing at him. Yemaja was a young woman of seventeen, an island beauty. She loved pleasure, and with a kola nut in her cheek she was laughing at everybody and everything. When she saw her husband among a group of men she threw her cloth open and danced across the road to a stranger, singing, 'In the oil palms, the father is looking for the mother flower, the mother flower is open, she waits for him.'

But the young husband did not like this joke, and coming up to her he commanded her to go home. Yemaja impudent in her confidence of her power over him teased him and meanwhile the family party turned a corner and Tanawe found herself in charge of Numi.

Two tall beautiful women stepped out of a house, and one of them said to Tanawe, 'Is this Numi, the son of Gani the Christian?'

Tanawe, seeing by the red and white marks on her face that she was a priestess, made a curtsey. The other woman offered Numi a honey cake. He was greatly alarmed, but not forgetting his duty he jerked his stomach towards her and piped, 'I am a man.'

She laughed and pressed the honey cake into his hand, then took him by the arm and tried to lead him into the house. He looked back and uttered a cry. Tanawe explained to the woman, 'Don't play with him, he doesn't like it.'

One of the women angrily pushed her away and told her to mind her own business. But Numi clasped Tanawe's hand, and she would not let go; she was now in charge of Numi. She knew how to take care of children because she had been trained in the art and she knew that it was a responsible task. She cried out, 'No, let him go, he doesn't like it.'

They pushed her away and pulled Numi into the house. Tanawe ran to tell her grandmother, but she found the old woman hurrying off as fast as she could, muttering and panting with fright.

Marimi knew very well what had happened to Numi, that was why she was running away. She and her family had suffered much already by their sons' various misconduct which had brought them into public notice. To become known, talked about, for whatever reason, is dangerous in Kolu. It attracts attention.

An injury was terrifying to Marimi because it made her feel conspicuous and open to attack from all sides. She was in such a panic that she could not look where she was going and tripped over the rough ground. When Tanawe, breathlessly pursuing, called out that some woman had taken Numi, she answered angrily, 'It's none of your business.'

'But he didn't want to go.'

'Hold your tongue, you naughty girl, or I'll beat you, and don't you tell anyone about those women or where they took Numi.'

'But, Grandma——'

Suddenly they heard screams and turning saw Ishe at the door of Moshalo's house. The woman was beating it with her fists and howling with rage.

Marimi, trembling with fright and anger, tried to call her daughter-in-law. 'The fool, the fool,' she muttered, and screamed at her, waving her bony arm; 'Come, come, you fool, be quiet, come away.'

But her voice could not reach the furious Ishe, and already people were beginning to stop and look. The old woman, moaning and twittering to herself, took Tanawe by the hand and ran home as fast as she could.

It was known to everyone in Kolu in a few minutes that the priestesses of Oke intended to give her a victim and all were pleased. They said that priests and priestesses were not quite useless. Now there was at least a chance of rain.

7 Ishe, failing to break Moshalo's door, ran to the headman of the town, Musa, who was eating his breakfast. Musa at once jumped up and seized his stick of office. He did not even wait to put on turban or gown, but shouted, 'Lead the way, woman, quick now.'

Musa called himself a Hausa and a Mahomedan, but he was three parts Kolua and very fond of strong beer. He was a small old man with a white beard, or rather a few scattered hairs waving from his chin which was almost hidden by the lower hanging lip. He was proud of his position as headman of Kolu and behaved with dignity like a great chief when he had nothing to do and his mind was at rest, but when there was a dispute or a fight anywhere in the town he came rushing to the place in a fluster, tripping over his gown, waving his thin arms, uttering cries of indignation which sounded like a duck quacking. He would often behave like this for a whole day, complaining to beggars and market women of the bad conduct of the Kolua people and his own troubles; until he suddenly recollected his importance and once more began to strut and glare.

Strangers to Kolu laughed at Musa, but this always surprised the natives who were not used to think him a joke. They had too much respect for his honesty and courage. Either from vanity or stupidity, Musa was not afraid of anybody, and he would charge a drunken mob single-handed and unarmed, quacking at them and making them fly before him. When Musa, closely followed by Ishe, who had now fallen behind him, came within forty yards of Moshalo's house, he began to shout, 'Hi, there, Moshalo, what's this?'

Moshalo, with the old priest Owule, came out and met him in the road.

'What do you want, grandfather?'

'Where's that boy? You give him up at once. Do you want the judge after you. Don't you know you can't take boys like that.'

'But I have taken him and I shall keep him.' She walked past him with her nose in the air, followed by her men, Ladile the wrestler, and Ajala, renowned among women for his powers. Moshalo was a dedicated priestess and had power to choose several husbands, and they washed her feet and served her on their knees.

Ishe began to shriek abuse, but Ajala catching her by the arm said, 'Is this the mother, we want her too.'

Musa began to lose his temper: 'What, are you mad? Ishe is wife to Gani the Christian. I tell you she'll go to the judge. You'll be strangled, you fool.'

Moshalo looking down upon the angry little man said contemptuously: 'What do you know about it? The mother has to give the child. It must be a gift. So we need the woman too.'

37

Owule was nearly blind, but he could hear by Musa's breathing that he was about to fly out. He put his hand on his sleeve and said in his mournful positive voice: 'We must do the right thing, chief. Suppose no rain come, all will die, Hausas and Muslims, too. If the white man punish us, we can't help that.'

'But the judge, the judge,' Musa shouted.

'Your judge, my dung,' said Moshalo; 'leave him to me,' and throwing forward her stomach and protruding her breasts, she walked away proudly and defiantly looking about her like a queen at the people, who avoided her glances.

It was just then that the party from the mission came up from the river. There was a stir in the crowd and a mob of labourers and canoemen who had surrounded the Christians on the shore broke a road for them among the country pagans. Makoto led the way, flourishing a stick and bellowing in Kolua, 'Make way for white man, priest of Jesus.'

Owule, Mashalo, and Musa himself, taken completely by surprise, did not know what to say or do and were pushed out of the way. When the procession had gone by Moshalo rushed after it, screaming, 'Kill the Christians,' but even Owule and Ladile dared not let her attack a white man, and they pulled her back. At the same time the mission party broke into the war hymn, 'Forward, Soldiers of Jesus,' and having finished the circuit of the pagan town returned across the market place towards the Hausa stalls.

8 By this time most of the respectable country people having performed their religious duties had gone home, and the market was filled with the local riff-raff, amusing themselves. But the mixed peoples of the Hausa and the boatmen's wards, though lawless among themselves, are not fanatical. They have

travelled and acquired curiosity and tolerance. They made way for the Christians and when Carr, choosing an open place between the meat market and the house walls, knelt down, a general silence fell upon them. The strange words (Carr spoke in English on purpose for experience had taught him that an English prayer was more likely to catch attention at once) excited their interest and voices were heard on all sides asking: 'What does he say, what is it, who is he?' and the replies: 'That's little long nose from Shibi, that's rat face,' and so on, various nicknames for Carr.

'What, is he a school white man?'

'No, he's a juju white man.'

'But what's he say, friends?'

Brimah, a Hausa carrier, employed sometimes at the mission, who was lounging in a quiet corner with a cigarette in his mouth, translated for those near him.

'He's asking the father god of the Christians to drive out Oke and all the Kolu gods.'

Carr, who felt the importance of his opportunity, was imploring God for help and inspiration. He clasped his hands and stretched them above his head, crying earnestly: 'Enlighten these poor people in their darkness and misery, O Lord,' and Brimah was heard: 'And now he's asking God to send the lightning on black men.'

But the market people having no one to point it out to them that they ought to resent the intrusion and curses of the foreigner looked on calmly. One woman remarked in a sympathetic tone that the white woman was too young to bear: 'Aie, she's only a little girl, and look at the size of her belly.'

'White women are all like that. They have no breasts and they're like little girls.'

'She has a neck like a sheep.'

'They're all like that,' said Brimah.

'I expect she has the fever.'

'Yes, she'll probably die soon. The last one at Berua died.'

'What are they doing now, Brimah?'

'They're praying for rain.'

'Do the Christians pray for rain?'

'Of course. If they need rain, they ask for it.'

This news gave great pleasure to the farmers, one of whom remarked: 'Our white man, old belly at Yanrin (this was Bradgate) he does nothing about it.'

A thoughtful old man, chief of the dyers, asked if the Christians had a rain-god.

'The father god does all that.'

'The Christians have only one god then?'

A little excited old man contradicted this: 'No, no, they have many. A score at least. In Lagos I saw a house full. Isn't that so, Brimah?'

Brimah answered carelessly: 'There are three gods: The Father, the Son, Jesus, and the Spirit.'

'What, is that the spirit which gets into Shangoedi?' a woman asked. Shangoedi was well known in Shibi for her fits.

'That's it,' said Brimah.

The woman, delighted to have the story to tell, turned to the others and explained. 'She told me about it in Shibi. The white mallam put his hand on her head. Then the bad spirit flew out of her nose in a sneeze and the good one went in at her mouth.'

'Well now,' said the dyer, 'about this spirit; is it like a wind, Brimah?'

'No, old cock. Sometimes it's like a fire, and sometimes like a white goat.'

'It's a spirit of madness.'

Brimah spat with good-natured contempt. 'All this is pagan talk. You're off the mark, friends. This spirit is simply God's Waziri. He does the dirty work, runs messages, chases after you when you don't do what you're told. I know because he

40

caught me one day at Shibi when I was drunk in a beer-house there. He jumped up my nose before I knew where I was. He was like a hot wind, and when he got inside me, he took me by the throat so that I nearly choked, and he said to me: "You damn bastard, Brimah, you're drunk. You go home now, quick. You repent to ma." '

Everyone was gazing at the big carrier with breathless interest. He spat, and looked round at them.

'What then, Brimah? Did you repent?'

He shrugged his big shoulders and tossed up his right hand. 'I did. Oh yes. I thought I wouldn't, but I did. I repented all right. Look here'—he pointed at a scar on his forehead—'that's where I repented. I cut my head open.' (Repent in Hausa means the action of bowing to the ground as well as the idea. The two are not distinguished.) Brimah wagged his head and grinned at his audience. 'I tell you, you can't make game of that spirit, friends. He's a nagger, if you like, a tough one.'

9 What made the best effect was the sermon. Illiterate people love to hear speeches, and especially stories. Besides, Ojo preached, or rather acted as interpreter, and Ojo had already become a name of power in Kolu. It was thought by many people that he and Carr between them had caused the drought.

The boy caught attention at once when he started forward, perspiring with excitement, his eye rolling, and held up a book. All books are magic and sacred objects in Yanrin where no one knows how to read them.

'Friends,' he shouted, 'listen to me. This is the truth. God wrote it himself in this book. This is God's book.' Ojo pointed with his left hand at the Bible and all eyes were turned upon it with awe and curiosity. An old man went down on his knees and bowed, and many others, feeling that this was a right thing to do, followed his example.

'Hear me, therefore,' Ojo cried; 'and every word, for it is true. Once upon a time God was angry with the people because of their badness. For you know that all people are born bad. So God was going to punish the people. But God had a Son, Jesus, who loved the people, and Jesus said to him: "These people are bad but I like them. I want to save them." '

'Then God said: "They have done wrong, therefore they must die, for that is the law." '

'Then Jesus said: "If I die instead of the people, will you forgive all these poor ignorant people?" ' (There was now complete silence in the audience and every face expressed close attention.) 'But God was still angry and He said: "No, that is not a fair offer. There are many people and you are only one." Then Jesus said: "But if I die slow, slow, with much pain, will that not do for many people?"

'But God was angry and said nothing. He did not answer Jesus. And all Jesus' friends went to sleep.

'Then Jesus gave himself to the wicked judge who ruled that country and they nailed his hands and feet to a wooden cross so that he died slow—slow—it was a day before he died and he felt such pain that he screamed all the time. (The people stirred and murmured in sympathy.) He screamed for a whole day, friends—the pain was worse than fire—but in that way he made God sorry. God was sorry. His anger was taken away. He felt good again and he said to Jesus: "All right, Jesus, you can die now and I forgive the people from hell. But you must go to hell, small, small." Then he put Jesus in hell. Then he took him out of hell, and made him a God and gave him a chair on his right hand. Now Jesus sits up there (he pointed to the sky), and if you ask him he will speak to God for you. He will ask God to forgive you and send you the rain.'

As soon as Ojo finished, shouts broke out from the party on

42

the Hausaside: 'What's that, Brimah? What's he say? What is it?'

They had heard every word and followed the story with the closest interest. It interested them so much that they wanted to hear it again, in order to find out what it meant.

Brimah, smiling with his nonchalant air, answered them: 'Why, he says that all you pagan people here are damn bad people and that's why God spoils your crops and stops the rain.'

'What!' said an old farmer. 'It's the white god has stopped the rain, is it?'

'That's it, papa. And unless you turn Christian and give God a good sacrifice like Jesus, you'll be starved out.'

'That's a fact,' said a woman with deep conviction, 'the white man's god is a fierce one. He's the strongest god in the world.'

Those near Brimah were attentive to the service because he could give them an intelligible account of it, but others further off, as soon as Ojo ceased speaking, lost their interest in events whose object they could not gather, and began to move about and to call to each other. The crowd at the back of the market place, on the Kolua side, were especially noisy. They threatened to drown Carr's voice while he was trying to explain in his slow Hausa why it was wrong and stupid to get drunk and commit fornication for any purpose, much more a religious purpose.

But old Musa, whose house was close by, now came rushing out as if from ambush, with his two men, crying in his shocked voice: 'Silence here. Get back, you scum. Have you no manners. Don't you see the white people, you blackguards.'

As soon as Musa had recovered from his astonishment at the mission people's arrival he had run to his own house in order to change into his best blue embroidered gown and a new indigo turban. Also he had caused his constables Salko and Fika to put on their best uniforms; gowns striped vertically in scarlet and white, each stripe a foot wide, and scarlet turbans as large as basins, two feet in diameter, surmounted on this hot morning by straw hats resembling gigantic chamber pots. Each man carried a two-edged sword, and a hard wood staff six feet long banded with iron above and below.

With his bodyguard Musa was prepared to do battle with the whole town, and rushed fearlessly to protect the Christians. His appearance restored order in a moment. Some of the foreign boatmen laughed at the old man, but they kept out of his reach.

But unluckily in his annoyance and anxiety he had already lost his dignity, and when he began to trot round the mission party, between it and the crowd, with his gown crooked and his turban slipping down his neck; first saluting the white man, then darting at interrupters with loud outcries, he made a bad impression on the Carrs, and especially Mrs. Carr.

Mrs. Carr had a strong suspicion of all persons in authority because it seemed to her unChristian for one person to be able to command others. This feeling like all her religious feelings was excited at the moment by worship and danger, and she said to her husband: 'Who is this horrible old man? What does he think he's doing. Do tell him to go away.'

Carr was also annoyed with Musa, because he considered that a missionary who accepted or seemed to accept protection from the state was in a false position and could not hope to obtain the people's confidence. He called out sharply to Musa: 'Go away, old man. We don't want you.'

Musa, astonished, unable to believe his ears, stared at him and then hastily salaamed.

Mrs. Carr waved her hand and cried impatiently, 'Go away, go away.' She could not bear the sight of the old chief; his anxious civility to the white people disgusted her even more than his abuse of the mob.

44

Some of these people understanding Carr's gestures sooner than Musa himself began to laugh, shouting: 'Go away, old man. The white man says, go away.' But Musa, conscious as he was of his energy, courage, and devotion to duty at great risk to himself, still could not believe that he was suffering a public humiliation before all the guttersnipes of the town. Luckily at this moment an excited girl, one of his own daughters, brought news that Ajala and the priestess Moshalo, who was even more reckless and fanatical than Ajala, were gathering the young men for an attack on the mission party. Musa rushed off immediately, uttering threats and curses at every step.

As soon as Musa and his guards ceased to keep the ring about the mission party the crowd flowed into it from all sides. They were bored with the service and wanted to go on with the feast day amusements. Also they had now recognized some of the party, although hidden in the back rows and disguised in clean mission jumpers, such as Makoto, the huge stupid labourer whose misadventures in the town had been a joke; Shangoedi the barren woman and lunatic, the terror of children, Nagulo the ex-convict, Umaru a deserter from three armies, French, English and German, whose body was covered with whip scars, and Aissa; and it amused them to see all the blackguards and idiots of the place rubbing shoulders with the white man and his wife. They did not know that to the Carrs, misery was a recommendation, and that Christ came to sinners.

'Hi, there's Shangoedi too.'

'Is she a Christian?'

'Isn't she rotten enough yet?'

'Sing for your chop, Aissa.'

This last sally shouted from the back of the crowd raised such a laugh as drowned the hymn.

10 Aissa was a well-known character in Kolu, where she had been at one time the most popular serving girl in Fanta's beer-house, famous for her noise and liveliness. But the girl was destined for ruin by her reckless goings-on, and no one had been surprised when she quarrelled with Fanta about the money she wasted on clothes and then bore a baby to a worthless fellow called Gajere, who was in gaol for the third time long before the child was born. This baby too turned out badly. It was a sickly little creature with a large umbilical hernia. It looked like a little angry old man, and everybody easily believed the gossips who said that it was a witch, that it had been born the wrong way round. Aissa was advised to put it out of the way. Fanta even offered to pay the necessary fees to have it destroyed.

But Aissa, in spite of advice and threats, would not give up the child. When it howled (as it did whenever it had the strength) she also bawled, and if anyone came near it she flew at him like a savage bitch. This did not surprise anybody, because devoted mothers are as common in Kolu as elsewhere. That kind of love is a natural thing, as cheap as air and water, and common to cats, bitches and hyenas. But everybody was surprised or indignant at Aissa's stupidity and violence.

She was the sort of girl who could not take advice and could not control herself like a sensible creature. She could not understand that her good days were over. Like a spoilt beauty she thought that the world must be turned upside down to give her sunshine at midnight. She demanded that Gajere should be ransomed from prison and that the evil spirit which had taken possession of the baby should be driven out of it. She ran to Yanrin and abused a member of Council who had her put in the stocks. She went to all the priests and mallams and juju

46

men for a hundred miles round and commanded them to give the baby medicine. She could not pay them but still she commanded, and when they refused she insulted them. Then their servants beat her and once more she spent a morning in the stocks.

The usual butt in country villages is an idiot or an epileptic, but Aissa had just as good qualifications as these because she could not hide her feelings. The stupidest could perceive the workings of her brain while she rushed from place to place, bewildered, incredulous, tumbling from one trouble into another, and always a worse one. Everyone except the youngest understood because everybody had suffered the same kind of misfortunes himself; but (what made the joke so good) not such violent ones and not so many. The man who has knocked his toe on a stone can't help laughing when he sees another do so and how much funnier it is when the other, having stubbed his toe once, immediately does it again and falls against a wall or into a dung heap. That's not only just like life but better than ordinary life.

All Yanrin and Shibi soon began to laugh at the very sight of Aissa's lugubrious astonished countenance usually decorated with a few bruises and a good deal of dirt. She was a boon to the children especially who knew that she was funny because their elders laughed at her. It was from the children that Ojo and Makoto had rescued her when they found her, too weak from fever and starvation to defend herself, being pelted in Shibi village. Ojo, always ambitious and eager in service, had recognized his opportunity, driven away the mob in spite of the abuse and threats of affectionate parents, and brought Aissa to the mission where from the first she had proved a quick and hard-working pupil. Three months of good food and success had given her back all her former looks and more than her former self-reliance.

11 Unluckily the market people who last remembered the girl as a butt were greatly amused to see her in the first row standing between the tall Nagulo and Mrs. Carr singing at the top of her voice. Aissa had been put in the front row because she was one of the best singers at the mission, and though she was looking anxiously at the crowd, turning her eyes from side to side to perceive some friend who could give her news of Gajere, she did not forget her responsibilities. The girl had inherited plenty of intelligence as well as strong feelings from her Fulani father and she had soon grasped the lessons of the Carrs. She knew that Jesus the Son of God was kind and loving, and that He desired her love. Every day after her rescue she had gone to the chapel, made Jesus a curtsey, and said: 'I tank you, Jesus, you good to me I good to you;' a practice which delighted Hilda. She was very angry with her husband when one day he described Aissa as making up to the Lord for her own ends—probably to get another husband bigger than the last or unlimited free beer. She was always angry when he made that kind of charge against her favourites, because it threatened her trust in them and in all the things she lived for. Therefore she did not believe it, and when during service she saw upon Aissa's upturned face, during such hymns as 'Lord Jesus, think of me,' or 'Jesus, our hope and hearts' desire,' a smile which might be called flirtatious, she told herself that the girl had a warm heart and sincere feelings.

In this she was right. Aissa had never ceased to be grateful to Jesus who had saved her from misery and her baby from the witch-finders, and she always sought to please him. At the moment she was bawling in her very best style. Her whole body kept time to the music, swaying at the hips, jerking at the knees and shoulder blades, so that the child Abba on her back was knocking its head against her spine. Having reached a verse which required powerful expression, she was singing with all her might. At the same time, as the hymn was a mournful one, she used the appropriate sad faces current at the mission. When she came to the verse in the Yoruba, which may be translated:

'All things I like best
I sacrifice to His blood,'

she rolled her head and eyes in most mournful fashion, raised her flat nose to the sky and opened and shut her big Cupid's mouth like a fish drinking.

'Hi, Totty,' the Kolua shouted, 'give us a pennyworth.'

Aissa looking at her book for the next verse and seeing on the way that some of the crowd were laughing at her, opened her eyes at them in a very coquettish expression, cocked up one shoulder and one hip in the classical pose of a charmer and grinned from ear to ear.

Of course she became at once serious and mournful again when the next verse started, but now and then her eyes darted another glance through the crowd. Even while she wagged her head at the climax of grief and the tears ran down the sides of her nose, it could be seen that she was looking out for old friends. She could easily do these two things at once because she was so well practised in hymn singing.

Suddenly she felt a poke in the ribs, jumped, stopped in the middle of a note and looked sideways, the tears still on her cheeks. Two of the girls from Fanta's beer-house, Hadesa and Fatu, with Fanta herself, were standing at the end of the row laughing at her. They had passed a long cane behind Makoto and Mrs. Carr, her guards on the left. Seeing that they had caught her attention they drew apart with waggish grins and showed just behind them a thick-set man, very black, with a mouth remarkable even in Kolu for its size, such that as he grinned at the girls and the crowd, he showed not only all his big teeth but his gums as well. But when his eyes fell

49

upon Aissa half his face was opened, he laughed so loudly that he was obliged to stop and shake his head from side to side.

This was the convict Gajere, and as soon as Aissa saw him she also was seized with laughter, bursting into irrepressible giggles. Then, shouting a greeting, she darted behind Mrs. Carr, pushed Makoto forward, and before he could catch her, dived into the crowd. This adroit movement brought her face to face with Gajere, whom, now that she was close to him, she addressed with proper modesty, murmuring shyly, 'Is it you?' Gajere was uttering cries of amazement, opening his eyes wide and raising both hands. Such gestures and cries were of course partly conventional. It was only good manners to use them in such circumstances. But Gajere was in fact delighted, his broken phrases were not entirely affectation, he really could not find words to express his joy and surprise. He had never seen Aissa so fat and good-looking even in her days of prosperity.

Fanta and the girls from the beer-house meanwhile were pressing round them, pushing them together, joking, fondling Aissa. Although they were chaffing the girl, they felt kindly towards her because she was enjoying her good luck. Everyone was pleased by her happiness. Her flustered grins caused the women such delight that they too were giggling helplessly and pushing each other.

Aissa wished to ask Gajere when he had been let out of prison, and to tell him she was glad to see him again, but every time she tried to speak she was seized with fits of laughter.

The women now turning their attention to the baby displayed their astonishment in recognizing Abba. How had she contrived to make him look so well. First they threw up their hands and eyes, amidst a chorus of the correct noises which resembled the squeaks of mice and the ululation of children being whipped, and then fell to chattering quickly together like monkeys who have found an important treasure.

As a further politeness, both to do themselves credit and please the now popular Aissa, they took the child from her back and passed him from hand to hand, with a thousand compliments:

'Aie, aie, see how fat he is.'

'Who cured him, Aissa?'

'Jesus.'

'Well, that's a wonderful thing.'

Gajere pushed his huge face close to the baby's and shouted: 'Hi, hi, little bridegroom, little swankpot.' Aissa wanted to warn them not to frighten the child. Just then Gajere put his nose in the baby's eye and Hadesa, who was holding him, made things worse by shouting at the man and jerking away from him. The child opened his mouth to howl. Aissa was frightened and rushed at them to take him away. But Abba, instead of uttering a howl, put out his tongue, rolled his huge lollipop eyes and hit himself on the nose.

There was another shout of laughter. Yemaja shrieked at the top of her voice: 'Look at him, then, did you see what he did?'

Aissa laughing too much began to crow and Fanta slapped her on the back and called for beer, but Fatu, one of her girls, had already gone for it. She came running now and offered the calabash to Aissa. Fatu had been one of Aissa's most constant enemies and detractors, but just now she loved her because of all the cries of affection, the smiles, the caresses of welcome which had infected her and everybody else in the neighbourhood with kind feelings and had spread sympathetic grins of pleasure through a whole section of the crowd.

Aissa shook her head. Christians did not drink beer. But immediately, seeing their looks of surprise and disappointment, she was ashamed of her rudeness, drank the beer, and turned up the calabash.

51

'That's the way,' they cried, delighted with her repentance.

The whole crowd surrounding them were dancing, shouting with laughter, jostling against each other; they were drunk with amusement and elation. Even those on the outskirts who could not see Aissa's face and did not know what was happening, were laughing while they shouted, 'What is it friends, what's the joke?'

The woman pushed Gajere against Aissa and Gajere, taking her hands, was bellowing into her face: 'Well, you've come back to us. That's good. You leave the Christians now. That's good. You come along with us. We'll make a feast. It's a wedding, friends. She's come back.'

12 The loss of Aissa put Carr into a difficulty because Mrs. Carr would not move without her, and meanwhile the whole party was obviously in danger from the crowd. The press was so thick that Musa could not get near them, and Mrs. Carr was several times pushed off her feet.

Carr called for volunteers to recapture Aissa, but Makoto and Ojo, who went together, brought back news after a long time that the girl had gone into Fanta's with Gajere and that she refused to come with them.

'I'm afraid she's a backslider,' said Carr to his wife. 'She's met this old flame and the excitement has been rather too much for her. In any case, we can't wait any longer.'

But Hilda, pale and furious, answered in her calm voice: 'Do what you think best, Harry, but I shall wait. I'm not going to leave the girl in Kolu.'

'My dear Hilda, do be reasonable. If you wait, you know we must all wait for you. And frankly things look ugly. You don't want to get us killed.'

'We're not going to get killed, and if we are, it doesn't make any difference. We might die any day of something.'

This was one of Carr's own arguments enforced in many a sermon and he could not refute it. Moreover, he could see that nothing could be done with Hilda who in her present mood was one of the most obstinate women in the world. Aissa's bad conduct, her ingratitude so unexpected, enraged her like a piece of treachery aimed at the heart of her faith, and she was quite ready to be martyred on the spot as a kind of protest against it or, as some might put it, in revenge.

But when Ojo, who was getting frightened, began to curse Aissa for a bad woman and a drunkard, she turned angrily upon him: 'How dare you speak like that, Ojo. Aissa is a very good girl; it's not her fault if she's cut off from us, and can't get back.'

'But, ma, she told me herself she——'

'I don't care what she said. She daren't say anything else while she's in the hands of those brutes.'

There was no reasoning with the woman. She was like a mother whose child disgraces itself in public; who is furious with the child and longs to be able to give it a good beating, but who is equally furious with anyone else who should dare say a word against it.

Carr had to be satisfied with allowing another search party, led by the old soldier Umaru, to push out towards Fanta's.

13 When Gajere and Aissa reached Fanta's they slipped away into the women's quarter and hid in the darkest corner of an empty hut. But they were now public property. The crowd with shouts and jokes hunted them through the compound, tracked them to their hiding place, dragged them out naked by the legs.

Aissa was ashamed, Gajere angry. He began to swear and wave his huge fists. Aissa protested and kicked. But all the people were enjoying themselves, laughing at them, caressing them; their jokes were friendly. It was impossible for Aissa to be angry with them while they felt for her and their flesh touched warm against hers. She began to laugh first, then to dance; Gajere lost his bad temper in making a joke so obscene that it let out his rage in the same explosion. The whole of the big compound was now crowded with the feasters, drinking, singing snatches of the Oke song, pretending to wrestle, fight, and make love.

Some while walking clapped their hands and sketched the movements of the ritual dance, jerking their hips, bending their knees, many of the younger men and women too eager and excited to wait for the drums, were dancing fiercely, leaping, squatting; the sweat ran down their backs, they were already in a trance, their eyes fixed, their muscles jigging like parts of a machine. They threw off their loin cloths and did not even hear the yells of encouragement from the crowd, who themselves carried away by the sight of them began also to leap, whirl, utter shrill cries which sounded like a defiance and an appeal. Not only the debtors, beggars, prostitutes, lepers, diseased wretches, ruptured children, syphilitic girls, idiots and outcasts, but those who seemed strong and well and to have no cares, leapt and grimaced with fierce, greedy cries and wild gestures which seemed to throw off heavy burdens of fear and anxiety; which said: 'I don't care for anybody, I don't care for anything. I'll do what I like this time.'

Only the old men and women with bodies twisted by work and disease, their grey faces hollow like rain-eaten stones, continued to look on, or pretending to join in, shuffled with bored, patient looks like those who perform a duty without much hope of profit.

Aissa danced like a mad woman. She seemed to herself not

only the happiest girl in the world but one of the most remarkable and powerful persons. In fact she was the most amusing dancer in the compound because as usual she was the liveliest, loudest, rudest, the most reckless. The other dancers crowded to her; took their cue from her, the watchers, especially old Fanta and the girls, clapped the time and encouraged her with loud cries.

Aissa was urged to greater and more extraordinary exertions. She leapt before Gajere three feet into the air, rocked before him on her haunches, beat herself against him and nearly threw him down; she felt that she could dance better and jump higher than anyone had ever done before; she screeched obscenities which seemed to her so amazingly and unexpectedly witty that she laughed until she choked.

The crowd, reeling with laughter, slapped at her and each other. Aissa swaying in Gajere's arms tried to speak to them, to make more jokes, but the very thought of them overwhelmed her with giggles.

Just then the mission party, struggling across the market place towards Fanta's in search of the lost sheep, met the main body of the pagans, and shouts were raised at the very door of the compound, 'Kill the Christians.'

Aissa cockahoop with joy yelled in answer: 'Silence, there, you bad people. Aren't you afraid?'

But the laughter had ceased. Everyone, even the drunkards, looked serious, some of the girls drew back from Aissa and Fanta said to her angrily: 'That's enough—we don't want any trouble in here.'

But Aissa cocked up her flat nose, struck a swaggering pose, and answered: 'I don't care for them, the bastards. We Christians are going to drive them all away.'

'Hold your tongue, you stupid girl.'

'Hold my tongue!' Aissa shouted. 'Why, I'm not afraid. I belong to Jesus now. It's the truth I tell you. We Christians are going to drive your Oke away. Then the rain will fall. Then all will be Christians. Then it will be the Kingdom of Heaven and Jesus will come. Then we'll all have plenty to eat and we'll have a good time always.'

Gajere, who alone continued to laugh at Aissa, gazing at her with wonder and delight as if he had never seen such a girl before, gave a guffaw and said: 'What, plenty of beer. Love, too.'

Aissa was annoyed with him. 'But it's true, you great fool, I swear it's true.'

'Yes, of course.'

An old farmer who had been listening with the blank face of a sheep now suddenly asked: 'What's this. Drive away Oke. What, no more rain.'

As if at a signal a yell went up from the thick crowd close to the door: 'Blasphemy.' Half the people in the beer-house hearing the pagan yell tried to push out of the compound while Moshalo's people outside were trying to break in. Aissa flung here and there in the press was still shouting at the top of her voice: 'But it's true, I tell you—it's true. It's in the holy book.'

The wall at one side of the compound, pushed off its foundations, fell down and the crowd surged in. Mashalo herself was seen, carrying her ceremonial whip like a sceptre, strutting forward; beside her old Owule led by one of his sons was talking very fast and angrily, though his words could not be distinguished. Moshalo was crying: 'Where's the one that cursed Oke.' A dozen voices shouted: 'There she is. It was Aissa.'

Aissa and Gajere were now standing alone in the empty middle of the compound. Aissa was astonished by the effect of her words. She had not been accustomed to see them so effective. She stared at the pagan chiefs with open eyes and mouth, then turned and fled into the hut to fetch Abba. When the child protested against her rough handling, she shook it

56

angrily: 'Be quiet, little fool. Haven't you got sense yet?' She bound it to her back with firm knots, in order to leave her hands free, and rushed out of the back door of the hut, making for the lane behind the compound.

But the pagans were swarming over the zana mats on that side also. She doubled back through the hut, and as she came out of the low door like a bolting rabbit Moshala's men yelled with one voice: 'There she is—catch her now.'

Aissa, perceiving that she was surrounded, stood up straight, took breath, and threw a glance of scorn upon the enemy. Then placing herself once more beside Gajere and raising herself upon her toes in the effort to make herself as tall as the priestess, she cried haughtily: 'Why, is it Moshalo? The diseased one, the liar. Her god is a lie too.' (Aissa said this to please her own god and win his support.)

'Hear her!' piped Owule, in horror and indignation, 'Hear what she says of Oke.'

'Don't you dare to touch me,' Aissa shouted, 'I belong to Jesus, the white man's god, and if you touch me he'll shoot his lightning at you.'

Intoxicated by her own bravery and grandeur she swaggered before them, nose in air, her back hollowed, and made an insulting gesture with her fingers: 'That's for you, you pagan dirt. Take care for yourselves. My god has stopped your rain, but soon he will send the fire too. That will teach you.'

Moshalo for her part was shouting the foulest women's abuse, and all her men equally furious waved clubs and swords, contorted themselves with rage; but none approached a step nearer Gajere and Aissa.

It is not usual in Kolu to begin a fight until each side has abused the other for some time, and no one cares to strike the first blow. This is a great responsibility because it makes a man noticeable and therefore exposed not only to reprisals but spells. Aissa was even more dangerous to attack than an ordinary person, because she had been in communication with the white man's gods; and Gajere was a brave fighting man.

Gajere, armed with a canoe paddle, did not shout abuse but laughed. He, like Aissa, was not afraid of the pagans, because he knew that Aissa was supported by a white man. He felt that by his connection with her he was a kind of official whom they would have to treat with circumspection. Moreover, he loved a fight which gave more excitement than drink. All his muscles danced while he strutted up to the foremost pagans and grinning said to Ajala: 'What is it, friend, do you want to see me.'

'No, it's that Christian witch we want.'

'That's my woman, friend.'

'We'll drive her.'

'What, and the white man too.'

'Yes, the white man.'

'And the soldiers perhaps.' Gajere laughed at the man and jostled him with his shoulder, then jumped back two yards to give swing for his paddle. Ajala also sprang back two yards and raised his spear. All the pagans, Aissa, Moshalo, Owule dancing from one foot to the other, screamed at each other.

'Burn her.'

'The white priest will curse you.'

'I'll kill you.'

'Bastard, punk, convict, rubbish.'

This furious contest of tongues went on for another three minutes until some person at the back of the pagans, unseen and therefore reckless and irresponsible, threw a piece of hard clay which passed close to Gajere's head. Gajere instantly rushed at Ajala and knocked him down with his paddle. At a second stroke he broke Ladile's teeth.

'You fight, you fight,' he shouted, 'I'm Jesus man.'

But just then a young man dodging behind him struck him with a hoe on his shaved skull. He fell like a bag.

Aissa when the fight began screamed for Fanta to take Abba away from her, for she imagined that the old woman was still close by, and tried to run round the house to find her. Then seeing Gajere fall she turned back and threw herself between his body and the mob. She implored them and cursed them at the same time: 'Friends, be careful, see, a man's fallen—God will curse you.'

Moshalo and Owule were pushing towards her. Old Owule between the priestess and his son was crying in indignant tones: 'Catch them, tie them up.'

One young man, seeing Gajere move made a chop at him on the ground with his matchet, cutting his arm; Aissa snatched up the paddle and flew at him with such a frenzy of rage that the crowd gave way before her; the young man threw himself down. The sharp paddle flew round her; it sparkled in the air like wheel spokes. Moshalo sprang out of its way like an acrobat; old Owule, blind and rheumatic, tottering forward without knowing where he was going, received a blow above the ear which knocked him senseless.

At this blasphemous act a yell of horror and rage broke from the pagans. A dozen spears were aimed at Aissa. Moshalo lashing at her with her manatee whip struck her in the face. Aissa was astonished by this cruelty to herself. She stooped down, covering her face with her hands, and cried out in reproachful tones: 'What are you doing? Be careful.'

The young man with the hoe aimed a blow at her neck, but she, as he raised his arm, darted under it and was gone before the angry warriors tumbling over each other could see where. She had dived through the broken wall into the crowded market place.

14 The same charge of the pagans which carried Fanta's house had broken the mission party into fragments. Carr and Mrs. Carr were tossed in opposite directions, Makoto was fighting in one corner, Umaru in another, Ojo and some of the women had taken refuge in Musa's house and the rest were scattered into ditches and holes.

Musa and his men plunging into the mass rescued the Carrs and took them to their boats, but when Aissa ran out of Fanta's, Umaru and his followers were still surrounded by a shouting mob, and Musa's house, defended only by his eldest wife, by another.

Everyone was gazing towards these two points of interest or running towards the waterside to see the missionaries carried away, so that Aissa, keeping her head low, might easily have escaped if some child wandering among the legs of the crowd and curiously observing objects at its own level had not cried out: 'Here she is, quick, quick, quick!'

All near looked that way, the pagans rushed out of Fanta's, and at once Aissa was seen racing madly along by the meat stalls.

Nearly everybody turned from the attack on Umaru to run after the woman simply because she was running away. Many as soon as they set eyes on her flying shape burst out laughing in enjoyment of the hunt.

Aissa, like most native girls of her age, was well built and a good runner. She could run as fast and stay as long as a man, and dodge quicker. Three or four times she doubled through her pursuers. A boy grabbed her by the cloth, but it stayed in his hands; she caught the baby out of its folds before it could fall and darted off in a new direction. She held the child before her with stiff arms, away from her body, as if it were a packet of butter. Half a dozen laughing boatmen pounced upon her from a corner, but their hands slid over her greasy back. A butcher cutting up a sheep with a matchet made a chop at her which should have cut her neck through, but she wriggled in the air like a jumping snake, and the blade only ripped her shoulder.

All thought her cut down, stopped running; and then saw her again leaping towards the waterside with a thin line of blood running down her spine and flicking from her tail bone. She was running faster than ever, with great leaps over the bumps in the ground and shrieking at every stroke of her legs: 'Oh Jesus, oh Jesus, oh Jesus!'

The crowds came running from the siege of Musa's house, from the shore, from Fanta's, from every corner; they hemmed her in on all sides and rushed together over the spot where she was. But when they got there she was lost. No one knew what had happened to her. All began to shout, wave their arms; panting they yelled at each other: 'She's gone—what do you think of that?' Ajala with a dirty rag glued to his broken head by its own raw skin, and Ladile with blood flying from his lips, were rushing to and fro with spears in their hands, howling contradictory orders and advice: 'Search the houses, to the river—burn Musa's, that's where she is.'

They asked everybody: 'Where is she, where did she go?' And if any answered, 'I don't know, I didn't see her,' they threatened to have him flogged, shouting, 'You were here, you must have seen her.'

One old woman answered: 'I didn't see her, but I saw a yellow bitch running down that lane.'

Ajala questioned her: 'Did the bitch look like an ordinary bitch?'

'No, I saw at once that she looked queer.'

'Had she blood on her shoulder?'

The woman could not be sure; she had not looked closely,

but after a little questioning she remembered that part of the bitch's back had a darker appearance than the rest, and finally that the patch had seemed to her very like blood. Cries of excitement and triumph burst out from the eager pagans: 'That's her. She's turned herself into a bitch. That's what we've got to look for.'

Aissa had dodged into Makunde's house, the only one on that side of the market place which possessed a Christian and might give refuge to her. Among the deep crooked lanes in Kolu, Makunde's was one of the deepest and narrowest. The roadway, a stream in the wet season, was like a ditch and the mat walls of the house hung over it from above like cliffs. It was entered from the market place by a steep bank down which Aissa had jumped as if into a pit. She flew round the first corner and into Makunde's porch before anyone had seen what had happened to her. Then before she could break in the door it was opened and Makoto whirled her into the compound. The hue and cry went past outside still in pursuit of the yellow bitch.

Makoto burst out laughing and exclaimed: 'Go on, you fools, run till you burst.' Makoto's family did not laugh. Old Marimi, Makunde, lame and asthmatic, were bustling here and there with looks of dismay; Yemaja was weeping; Tanawe, who had been beating corn with a child's pestle and mortar, continued to work because she had not been given any other task, but she knew well that a disaster had fallen, and gazed with frightened eyes at Makoto and Aissa, so that the pestle struck from side to side against the hollow wood.

Makoto was not a popular member of the family. He had been a burden and a nuisance to them for years and then a disgrace. But it did not occur to anyone to deny him a refuge; even to Yemaja, who was moaning: 'They'll kill us all, they'll destroy us.'

When Yemaja saw Aissa she caught up a pestle and flew at her. 'Out with you, trash. What have you to do with us?'

But Makoto snatched away the pestle and exclaimed: 'What, you wicked woman, you'd have her killed then, would you?'

'What have we got to do with her?'

But old Makunde staggering by, with a huge zana mat on his shoulder, muttered to her: 'Be quiet, girl, not so much noise.'

'See whom he's brought in, the worthless fellow.'

Makunde peered out of his little bloodshot eyes at Aissa and said, 'Who then?'

Makoto, inclining his huge body in respect towards his father, and yet speaking to him carelessly, for was he not a Christian and Makunde an old pagan, began to explain: 'You understand, Daddy, she's a friend of mine, a holy woman.'

'It can't be helped now,' the old man muttered; then calling to Marimi, 'Granny there, bring that sleeping mat, the old one.'

He sent Yemaja to watch in the road lest the search party should return on their tracks.

Marimi was silently weeping in despair and fright even while she worked. She hobbled here and there gathering mats, rags, anything to cover the fugitives; every moment she groaned: 'Oh, what a misfortune.' But when she saw Makunde she shouted angrily at him: 'Where have you been then, hurry up. There's no time to lose, I should think.'

She flew for Makoto: 'Come on, then; dear, what a misfortune. What's this woman, very well then. It doesn't matter. Go on with you, hurry up.'

She hurried them from the hut through the inner compound to the farthest corner of the house where behind the latrine there was a ditch half full of rubbish. Here she made them lie down and she covered them with the mats and a thin sprinkling of dry earth.

The two old people were still busy at their task when a man's voice was heard calling from the lane: 'Did you look in Makunde's?'

Terrified, stumbling together in their fright, they hurried towards the gate.

But the search party had entered the next house, that of a dyer called Ishola, who could be heard already crying out that he had not even seen a Christian. 'Try Makunde's,' he shouted. 'I shouldn't be surprised if Makoto slipped in there.'

'It's the woman we're after.'

'Well then, she isn't here.'

'We're destroyed,' said Marimi to her husband. 'It's a misfortune certainly.'

A mat between the two houses was pushed down and Ladile himself walked in. But he had not expected to come upon the old people. Ladile belonged to a good family, he admired himself for his manners. He stopped, saluted, and murmured: 'Pardon, father, pardon, mother. I was seeking a Christian woman who struck Owule.'

'Oh, the villain,' cried Marimi in horror and disgust. 'Did she strike Owule?'

'We saw a girl run past here a little while ago,' said Makunde.

'They say she has changed herself into a bitch.'

'A bitch. Why then, I saw a bitch going down there as fast as she could run, and crying all the way,' said Makunde.

'Which way, father?'

'This way, sir, this way.' Makunde took Ladile towards the porch. Marimi, catching sight of Tanawe, ran to her and giving her a hard shake by the arm, whispered angrily: 'Now you run to the judge quickly and tell him to send police because they're killing the Christians. Speak to him yourself so that he will hear.'

'The judge, Granny?'

'Yes, you little fool. He's at Akoko. Run now. Straight to himself.'

She pushed Tanawe out of the gate. Ladile and Makunde were still standing there, and Ladile turned round, but Marimi said to him, smiling and curtseying: 'I'm sending the child for a message.' She could not think of what she could give for an excuse. But Ladile paid no attention to her. He shouted for his men to look again in all the holes towards the waterside: 'For Makunde here has seen a bitch with a bloody back and she went down by the water.'

Tanawe was already in the market place, which was crowded with drunken dancers and the blackguards of every neighbouring town, irresponsible strangers who did not care what local people thought of them. Most of them, men and women, had already thrown away their clothes; their drunken yells and furious gestures as they danced and wrestled were more like gestures of hatred than love. But Tanawe, threading her way among them, was too much preoccupied with her task to be afraid or even to notice her danger. The very notion of speaking to the judge, who was a greater man than the Emir or even Musa, made her tremble.

Confusion of mind and terror made her feel like a different person with a different body and different legs over which she had little control. Sobs burst from her, pumped out at each step as she ran, and she thought: 'Something terrible is going to happen to me.' But her grandmother's confidence in her quality was not unfounded, her legs continued to trot towards the Akoko road, and even in her mind, which still belonged to her, she never thought of giving up her enterprise.

For one thing she had to do what she was told, and for another she would have been ashamed to fail in an important grown-up task. Tanawe had been trained to consider virtue those qualities which being equally valuable to parents and admired by the world that also profits by them are virtue everywhere. She had learnt to be dutiful and to serve a common purpose. She knew that it was shameful to fail in one's duty, to be a coward, to be mean or selfish, and this knowledge enforced by example and teaching and many slaps, had reached every part of her body so that her legs were now conducting themselves with great bravery while her mind was not so brave.

15 Akoko is five miles from Kolu along the bush road, which winds like the path of a maze through low woods. The track is hollowed out by the rains and crossed at every yard by thick roots; in several places it mounts a rock as steep as a roof, and then at once falls into a deep hole in which, during the rains, a traveller might easily be drowned.

In the rains it is a blind road. No ten yards are straight and the elephant grass seven foot high stands like a thick hedge on each side. But after November, when the hunters burn the grass to drive the game, the track is clear for some distance in each direction. Its cream sand and yellow clay stand out like paint on the black ground, covered with soot and ash; it can be seen forty yards away winding beneath the branches of the trees, dwarfed and distorted by many fires, whose trunks are like artificial models in coal.

This road was not planned. It was made directly by the feet of the travellers going from one place to another, taking a big curve at the first mile round Kolu hill, which is full of leopards, and another at the third to avoid a tree which has been known to harbour demons. Lions have been seen on this road which skirts the central forest of Yanrin, two thousand square miles of uninhabited bush, and leopards more dangerous than lions have sometimes killed a solitary trader there. Men do not care to travel it alone. But they are much more afraid of the demons than of the leopards.

Many of the trees are haunted and there are two ruined villages close by the road; both crowded with the spirits of their dead, buried there long ago and malignant with jealousy and spite against all people still alive in this happy and interesting world.

Tanawe's terror of the demons was such that from the moment when she ran through the gap in the old Kolu wall and found herself alone in the black woods she became quite stupid and drunk. She scarcely knew what she was doing. She trotted forward like an automatic toy, her eyes bulging from her head, her mouth open, loud moans bursting from her chest. A demon was waiting for her at the very first village. She saw it dodging from one tree to another and turned round and ran for her life. At every step she expected to feel it's teeth in her back. But when she had run twenty yards she remembered her grandmother's command, her heroic legs turned her round, and shutting her eyes, squeaking like a rat, she scuttled past the ambush.

She ran then until she fell exhausted, fainting. But when a family of kola-nut traders, father, mother, sister, and two children, hurrying to Kolu to sell at good prices during the feast, revived her with massage and cold water, her first words were: 'Is this Akoko?'

When she saw them, strangers, bending over her, she was frightened of them, and began to cry: 'I'm going to Akoko.' They put half a nut in her mouth and set her on the road, but she ran off without saying thank you.

She reached Akoko with cut feet and a thin, alarmed countenance, like one who had passed through a bad night, but she did not feel tired because her whole body was engaged with the problem, how to see the judge, what to say to him.

16 Petitioners usually found it easy to see Bradgate because he made a rule that when he was on trek anyone could approach him at any time. This is a common practice in Nigeria because any other leaves to the office staff, messengers, orderlies, the power to choose who shall see the magistrate and who shall not and the opportunity of charging for the privilege.

Marimi herself had once stalked Bragdate in his bath in order to complain against her tax assessment; Tanawe therefore had been told to go directly to the judge wherever she saw him.

Unluckily when she came to Akoko she found the place crowded with almost the whole native administration, who seemed to bar every path.

Akoko camp is on the bank of the Akoko river. The rest house, of the dumb bell type, two round huts joined by an open verandah, stands near a big baobab at about thirty yards from the river and twenty from the road. It faces the river and the official flagstaff, a tall crooked branch on a living tree which overhangs the stream. The servants' huts and stalls lie behind the house on a by-path from the main road before its expansion into the clearing. The house is therefore alone and convenient for approach from any direction. But on this afternoon the main road was blocked by stallions, which, circling, neighing, rearing at each other, frightened Tanawe even more than the tall dogarai of the guard, dressed in their state parti-coloured robes of red and white and crimson turbans, who stood on every side, leaning on their six foot muskets and glaring fiercely at everybody that came near them.

In the grass behind the guards squatted the humble elders of Akoko, waiting to pay their respects to their chief; beyond, in the clearing itself, between the tumble down rest house with large holes in its thatch and the bare river bank, the Emir in a

68

blue turban and gown could be seen on his state carpet, the Treasurer on one side, the Alkali (judge of the Mahomedan court) on the other, seated also, but without carpets; and behind, standing up, a crowd of minor officials and guards. Besides the Emir and a little forward, an old man, resembling the Emir himself with his thin nose and little white beard, dressed like him in the robes of an important person, but older and plainly decrepit, was prostrating himself over and over again before the white man, who seemed to be in a very bad temper.

Tanawe perceived that this angry person was the judge, only because the old man, whom she recognized as the Sarkin Tafirki (minister or chief of roads) was repenting before him. She had seen one white man before, Carr of the mission, but he was small and thin and his face was literally white; this judge was fat, his face was red, his nose was even purple. Moreover, Carr usually wore beautiful white cloths, but the judge was dressed in worse clothes than his own servants. His hat was broken, his dirty, khaki shirt was torn at the pockets, his trousers had a huge patch of flour bag on the seat and another inside each knee, his native riding boots were trodden over, his spectacles were mended with string and sealing wax. These disgraceful boots and trousers moreover were soaked with mud to mid thigh and his thick bare arms to the elbow; there was mud even on his face, and it dripped from him as he jumped from the box on which he was sitting to snatch up a piece of timber lying before him. 'Look at this,' he shouted in Hausa. 'What is it, what is it good for? Do you call this iron-wood? The ants are eating it already.'

The Emir, a dignified old gentleman, raised his hands and eyes as if to say, I will agree to anything, anything, but pray do not make a scene. The old Sarkin Tafirki once more salaamed to the earth and cried in his broken voice, 'Lord, lion, master.'

17 The Sarkin Tafirki was a new minister. Three months before Bradgate, having asked the Emir to tea, had suggested that a bridge over Akoko joining the Yanrin roads to the great Yoruba cities of Oyo and Ibadan, would double the trade and wealth of the country. The Emir answered that his lordship spoke nothing but truth and wisdom; a bridge was most desirable.

Bradgate had then asked the Treasury for a grant. But the Treasurer answered that a permanent bridge would cost a thousand pounds; much more than they could afford in a poor place like Yanrin. In this the Treasury did its duty, which is not to produce wealth or advance the welfare of the people but to scrape and hoard; and to invent new obstacles in the way of officials who desire to spend anything.

For the Treasury roads, bridges, hospitals have nothing to do with trade or humanity, but are counters in a game. The Treasury won this game in Yanrin and scored a thousand pounds. But the drought laying bare the bed of the river gave Bradgate a chance of building a temporary bridge, to last perhaps ten years, at a cost of twenty to thirty pounds.

The Treasury refused the thirty pounds on the grounds that the Public Works department did not approve temporary bridges.

The P.W.D. has a different function from the Treasury. Its job is to fight for money as hard as it can. But it must prevent any other department such as the political or the military from works which might otherwise be carried out by itself.

In this warfare which breeds a race of the hardiest letter writers and most brilliant obstructionists in the world, a bush officer like Bradgate, enthusiastic about his schemes, sentimental about his pagans, had no more chance than a curate among the city sharks. He was diddled all round and made to look like a fool.

He not only did not get his thirty pounds, but was asked to explain an overpayment of three pounds three and fourpence on native markets or alternatively to refund the money.

He refunded the money and cursed the government. Then by seizing upon a whole year's allocation for dogarai uniforms and extra services, with five pounds out of the pay of an assistant roadman not yet appointed, he collected twenty pounds for the bridge. The rest he advanced from his own pocket against next year's vote for capital works.

But now having expended on his bridge already in six weeks a year's nervous energy and risked a prosecution for forgery and the embezzlement of public funds, he was summoned to Berua on a boundary commission. He sent for the Emir and said: 'This work must be begun at once. Who is the best man to take charge of it?'

There was no minister of transport in Yanrin. His duties were neglected by Mallam Illo who, as a writer of Ajmi (the Latin characters) was busy every day with census and tax.

'We want a whole time man on the job,' said Bradgate.

For the first time the Emir, moved out of his habitual resigned melancholy in which all events and all projects appeared equally boring and trivial, gave his mind to the business in hand and exclaimed with animation: 'Yes, Lord, most certainly we do. A minister of roads. I shall seek him at once. In Yanrin the minister of roads gets three pounds a month.'

'I think we could give four to a really good man with experience of the work.'

'Yes, indeed. Four, or even five.'

'Four would be enough, don't you think?'

'Lion, I most certainly think so.'

71

The Emir was delighted. For a long time he had been troubled for the sad condition of his old friend and follower Haji Suli, the companion of his vigorous youth.

Haji Suli was one of the most honourable and respected men in Yanrin, a Mecca pilgrim, a veteran who had fought under Nagwomachi of Kontagora in a hundred slave raids; a man whom long practice in religion had rendered incapable of a mean, cowardly or undignified action; but at seventy-five or more, injured by disease and hardship, and unprovided with sons or active wives to support him, a pauper.

The Emir, like other Emirs, looked upon himself as the father to his people, and would have been ashamed to turn anyone from his doors. His palace was crowded with parasites and he was three years' pay in debt. He gave Suli house room, clothes and food, but he was still wounded every day in his deepest feelings by the sight of such a good and worthy man in poverty and dependence, with but one servant and no horse.

But now God to whom he offered his heartfelt thanks had spoken to the judge and bent him to His service. He rode back to Yanrin with a joyful heart, called his councillors, and said to them: 'By God's will we have a place worthy of the Haji. He shall be minister of roads.' The council as always did not agree at once, and meanwhile applications came from all Yanrin, Berua, and even towns as far away as Zaria, from men of the greatest honour and influence, prepared to pay fifteen and twenty pounds down in coined silver for one of the richest posts in the administration. For a minister of roads makes almost as much as a district head or a tax mallam. Every villager who wants exemption from road work, every manager of a caravanserai who wants to avoid an audit, every blacksmith with tools to sell, or farmer with grain and beer, and every village chief who desires to avert a bridge or divert a road, comes with his present.

72

Each of the council had his candidate with ready money jingling in a bag, but the Emir Jibrim was not the kind of man to be corrupted by a bribe. The richest gift never moved him from his principles. He appointed Suli and, moreover, he persuaded Bradgate that there was no better man to be had.

Bradgate carefully explained his plans to the Haji. 'Here,' he said, 'is a list of all we want. How long will it take you to collect this material and these men?'

'A single day, your lordship. Before to-morrow all shall be there.'

'Take a fortnight and make sure.'

Three weeks later on his return from Shibi, Bradgate, at leisure for the bridge, asked if all was ready, and the Emir's messenger answered that all was ready to the last nail. For so the Emir had been assured by Haji, who had asked his servant who had asked the foreman who had sent his wife to Akoko village who had asked several other ladies, friends of hers, and frequent visitors to the river.

Then Bradgate, with the Emir, the Haji, the council, the guards, a police escort, twenty-seven women married, and five independent, a hundred and forty carriers with grain, food, kola-nuts, chickens, tools, chairs, mats and beer, went to build the bridge and found awaiting them half a dozen rotten sticks pulled out of some house roof, a coil of rope, a hundredweight of stones, two mats, and a deputation of ferrymen ready to prove by irrefutable logic that the Akoko could never be bridged. It was too deep, too wide, too swift, too muddy; and above all, none had ever bridged it before.

Bradgate had fifteen years' service in the army, much of it spent in West Africa, and ten in the political service. He prided himself upon knowing the native, upon his powers of tact, patience and sympathy and acceptance. He was fond of saying that a political officer needed eyes and ears all round him, blind

73

eyes and deaf ears; and six men's enthusiasm for taking things easy, but he had given his heart to the Akoko bridge. He had already drafted a scheme for two new roads with government inns, and four new markets, to be served by the great southern trade route and the bridge. He had therefore lost his temper with the whole native administration.

'What's the good of you?' he shouted at them. 'What are you for? How can anything be done for you if you won't do a damn thing for yourselves. What's the good of being sorry now. It will take weeks to get hard wood in thirty-foot sticks and the rains may break to-morrow. What on earth do you pay Sarkin Tafirki for if he can't take the trouble to do the job that any small boy could do?'

The Emir was perspiring with distress. He waved his small beautiful hands in the gesture which said: 'Do anything you like, but pray change the subject now.'

Every face in the clearing, even the faces of the small dirty boys holding the horses and the villagers in the grass, wore the same look of humiliation and impatience and scores of blood-shot eyes glared at Bradgate with hatred and wonder. Why was he making this fuss? Why was he punishing them with his anger? What did it matter if the Akoko was never bridged?

'You know this is a big thing,' Bradgate exclaimed, growing more and more indignant and plaintive; 'you know that Yanrin is poor though the woods are full of shea nuts that anybody can pick up, you know that in every bad year people are short of food, you know that the only thing that keeps out the trader is the want of a safe road with bridges, and now when there is a good chance of one you throw it away.'

'Lord, lord, timber is here; at least we can begin.'

'But I tell you these sticks are not only of soft wood but they are too short.'

Bradgate drew breath, controlled his temper, telling himself that the people were unfamiliar with trestle bridges and unused to picture any kind of construction in their minds since they never saw pictures of anything. He described once more how he meant to build the trestles as tall as the deep banks of the river, with their legs sloped outwards like a man resisting the current. 'But I'll show you,' he cried, and taking up a still longer pole, the measure of the trestle legs, he rushed down into the bed of the river.

The Emir, the Haji, the old Alkali and their followers, all dressed in their best, hastened after him with polite bustle but with looks of disgust and boredom.

The Akoko at this place was normally about eighty feet wide and thirty deep, but now the tall banks stood dry from top to bottom and the river bed had become a narrow brook trickling through muddy pools at the bottom of the chasm.

Bradgate rushed down the steep banks and waded into the mud, which spurted over his arms and face. He was compelled to raise his knees almost up to his chin in order to make each step, an exercise for which a man of his age and bulk was not fitted; so that he was soon panting for breath. The sweat poured down his face. He was a ridiculous object.

The Emir and his statesmen did not enter the mud. They would rather have died than have been obliged to perform such vulgar antics; they stood on the shore raising the edge of their robes, and the Emir cried in his shaky voice: 'Lord, lion, pray be careful. Lord, it is not necessary, I understand you.'

The Emir and the Alkali were distressed to see a white man and a ruler making such a despicable object of himself, but the lesser men in the court, not so noble in feeling, did not disguise their disgust and contempt. What increased that disgust was the fact obvious to them all that the white man did not care, perhaps did not even know that he was disgracing himself. 'See,' Bradgate shouted, having at last struggled into mid-stream, 'this is half-way. Now look,' he planted his long bamboo and worked it into the mud. 'Look there' (pointing up) 'it is not a foot too long. For consider, when the weight of the bridge is above the legs will sink still further. Now do you understand why we must have long sticks.'

Now the courtiers on shore dared to speak among themselves. A voice was heard: 'Allah, who wants a bridge. It will only bring a lot of cursed Yoruba traders.'

'Yes, to spoil the people and bring disease among them.'

Yerima, chief pagan member of the council, an old and respected elder but bad tempered and excitable, exclaimed: 'Look at Berua, how it has been ruined by the traders. A decent man or woman cannot go there for fear of being swindled or insulted by some dog from the white man's towns. And now they want to spoil Yanrin too.'

Another voice, that of the chief eunuch, a veteran and a cynic, murmured: 'You need not fear, Yerima, the bridge won't last long. The first bush fire will eat it.'

'Yes, or some other fire,' said Yerima, who was reputed to have burnt at least one bridge with his own hands.

Bradgate was shouting still, and his voice seemed now to implore them to show a little intelligent interest in his plans for their advantage. 'Since the leg will slope thus it must be taller than the bank; there now, you see' (pointing upwards and at the same moment almost sitting down in the deep slime) 'and two of that length are wanted for each pair of legs, that is fourteen in all.'

Tanawe had been running here and there seeking a way through the crowd. She repeated every moment her parrot cry: 'News, news, for the white man.' But no one paid any attention to her until one of the ragged tail which follows a native court wherever it goes, to wait on servants and the servants of servants, a thin handsome young man carrying a tin jerry in his hand and a broken kettle among the tatters on his back, irritated beyond patience by Bradgate's persistence, aimed a savage blow at her and told her to be off.

'But I want to see the judge. I have important news. They're killing people in Kolu.'

'I don't care for that. Go off with you.'

But Tanawe's eye had fallen on one of Bradgate's servants, a small boy who, in a clean vest and khaki shorts creased at the sides, was walking along the road swinging a bottle.

She was delighted to see at last one of her own size and one whose good-natured expression promised help. The small boy, unlike everybody else in sight, was in good spirits. He was singing as he walked, no doubt for the ears of the guard, a song imputing various scandalous vices to Bradgate:

'The girls come to the court house and smile at Belly
They let their clothes fall off, thrust their hips sideways
Why does Belly keep no wife.
Why does he refuse the most beautiful girls,
Is it because he is poor, no, he is rich with the taxes of the poor.
He has silver and nickel, horses and clothes.
Is it because he is impotent
No, because he is more powerful than a horse.'

Tanawe, interrupting the fourth and most scurrilous verse, planted herself in front of the small boy and made him a curtsey.

'I want to see the judge.'

'There he is, in the mud.'

'But I can't go there because they won't let me.'

'No, of course not. You can't go by yourself. No one is allowed to see the judge like that. What do you think. First you must ask one of the judge's people.'

'Could you take me?'

'I'm busy, but I could get someone to take you if you have the cash.'

'Must I pay?'

'Of course.'

'But how much?'

'Sixpence.'

'Sixpence?' Tanawe was astonished.

'Most people pay a shilling,' said the small boy carelessly.

Such sums amazed Tanawe. A shilling in Yanrin is equivalent to ten in England. She made a face and began to cry. The small boy consoled her: 'Cheer up, don't cry, woman. I'll do what I can for you. How much have you got?'

Tanawe had two anini (an anini is one-tenth of a penny) and five cowries (cowries in Kolu are 150 to the penny) in a bag purse slung from her neck. She offered this sum with diffidence. But the small boy accepted it and then pointing his bottle towards the kitchen said: 'Go there and ask for Jamesu. He will take you to the judge.' He strolled off. Tanawe ran to the kitchen where she found a little crowd of servants and their friends surrounding a big fat Yoruba, dressed like a white man with glittering shoes on his feet and a green felt hat tilted over his left eye. This was Jacob or Yacubu, cook to the company's agent at Shibi. He often visited Bradgate's household to see his friend Jamesu, Bradgate's head boy, and Mr. Williams, the clerk. These three, Christians from the coast, regarded themselves as the only civilized persons in Yanrin.

18 Jacob was in good form. He was making one joke after another and keeping all these people in fits of laughter. They were laughing so heartily when Tanawe came up to them, bowing, trembling, whispering in her small voice, 'Lord, master,' that none of them saw her.

Jacob was popular with everybody not only for his jokes and his friendliness, but for his generosity, his loyalty as a friend, his complete lack of snobbery. He had a great respect for himself, but it was founded on a reasonable basis for he practised all the virtues and possessed all the accomplishments which were most admired by the lower rank of traders among whom he had been bred.

He did not judge anyone hardly and forgave very readily because he valued himself as a man of the world whose axiom it is that all men and women, given the chance, are capable of any crime or vice. He did not lay up wealth for himself because he did not want money to keep, but to spend, and he was charitable to a fault. He enjoyed giving away as much as he liked a drink or a woman.

His accomplishments which he fancied to be those of every white man were to drink raw whisky and gin without blinking, and to invent on the moment such lies and explanations as were calculated most surely to hide the defects and exaggerate the worth of any article the subject of bargaining. Jacob knew that it was contemptible in any man to hesitate at any trick or lie in the course of business. Business was like war, and it was a war of every man and woman against each other. Jacob told with the pride of a soldier who has laid some good ambushes in his time the tricks by which he had cheated people.

When Tanawe saw Jacob she knew at once by his easy attitude, his dignified gestures, his broad nonchalant grin that he was the greatest man present and made to him her curtsey.

'Well, little girl,' said Jacob in a kind voice.

Tanawe said that please she wished to see the judge.

Jacob who in the fashionable coast style gave all his conversations with inferiors a cynical or humorous turn, laughed and mimicked her to Jamesu the cook: 'She wants the judge, Jamesu.'

Jamesu, who affected the same high class jaunty air, cried, 'What, you bad girl, want to be his woman, do you?'

'No, I want to see him on business, because they're killing people in Kolu.'

'You come and see me on business,' said Jacob, catching her arm: 'You come into the bush and I'll do your business.' This joke made all laugh.

But Tanawe repeated, 'I want to see the judge, people are being killed in Kolu.'

A Hausa boy cleaning harness in the kitchen door said that she could not see the judge because he was busy. 'He can't see everybody, can he?'

'But I've paid.'

All the servants burst out laughing, and Jacob asked, 'What did you pay?'

'I paid the small boy.'

'I'll take you for a shilling,' the house boy said.

'But I gave all to the small boy.'

'Get out then.'

'You like me?' said Jacob, pinching her chin.

Tanawe, nearly crying, curtsied and said, 'Yes.'

This made them all laugh, and Jamesu, hastening to accord his manners with Jacob, gave him a waggish poke in the ribs and said, 'You bad boy—I know you.'

'You come and tell me all about it,' said Jacob, taking her by the arm and drawing her into the bush. He pulled off her upper cloth and caught hold of her. Tanawe, shocked and frightened, cried out and tried to run away. Jamesu appeared and laughing exclaimed, 'What you do, you bad boy?'

'You go away, Jamesu, we got business.'

Tanawe uttered a yell which frightened both the boys; Jacob gave her a shake and said, 'Be silent, you little trash.'

'Call the policeman,' Jacob shouted, and he said to Tanawe, 'Now you're going to be whipped.'

But at this moment the house boy said, 'Take care,' and disappeared into the bush. Jacob and Jamesu turning round faced Bradgate, who, covered with mud from head to foot and scarlet with anger and exertion, glared at Jamesu and said, 'Tell boy bring bath one time.'

Tanawe threw herself at the judge's feet and embraced his boots; the two boys overcome with terror also began to stoop as if expecting the catastrophe actually to fall upon them like a blow on the head.

But they had no need to be afraid because Tanawe, like other children, had forgotten their offence the moment it had ceased. She had now only one idea in her head, to disburden herself to Bradgate of her message.

'Lord,' she piped, 'they're killing people in Kolu. Marimi sent me.'

'What, what,' said Bradgate; 'what's she want?'

Jacob, straightening his back, securing his self-possession in a moment, exclaimed, 'Sah, she wish to tell you the pagans in Kolu make palaver, dey fight, dey all drunk. Dey kill some Christians come from Shibi.'

'That's it,' said Tanawe.

'Killing Christians from Shibi?'

'Yes, sah.'

'But is this true?'

'Oh yes, sah, I come myself to tell you, but I no fit catch you. I tink you send police.'

'Ibrahim, why wasn't I told of this—tell the Sarkin Dogarai to send six mounted men to Kolu.'

'I try to tell you, sah, long time. I run all de way from Kolu. I tink you should hear.'

'Oh did you. Hurry up with my horse, Maidoki.'

'I very tired, sah. I break my shoe when I run.'

Jacob knew very well that Bradgate did not believe him, but his maxim in dealing with what are called in Nigeria judgy white men, that is, magistrates, officers, doctors, was to be as impudent and troublesome to them as possible. For he knew that the law forbade them to strike him or even to remove him by force, and he did not respect anything but force.

Grinning from ear to ear he followed Bradgate, his hat tilted over his ear, crying: 'I help you, sah. I run all de way fo you, sah. You no give me something, sah. I think you give me dollah. I run for you, sah, because I say, if dem Christians done get killed someone go write paper in England, write prafs parliament member, den ma frien Mister Bradgate catch big trouble.'

Bradgate was getting on his horse. At this remark he glared down at the bold Jacob with an expression which made the man, fortified as he was by his education, draw back a step.

Jacob did not lose his confidence, for he knew that he was safe, but he adopted a new plan of attack.

'Look, sah!'—he held up his shoe—'my good shoe come from home (England) all broke, sah, when I run fo you.'

Bradgate on his side had had time to recollect one or two cases in which coast natives even more mean and impudent than Jacob had made serious trouble for political officers by writing garbled stories to papers or even to M.P.s at home, and that such cases were apt to do harm to the whole service as well as the officers. Bradgate was a good political officer, that is to say he never forgot that his job was politic—to make the best of given circumstances whatever they were, including such as Jacob, parliamentary careerists, the power for harm of stupid and prejudiced people of all kinds, as well as witchcraft and the weather.

He therefore suddenly changed his expression to a bland smile, and said, 'Thank you, Jacob, I know we can always rely upon your sense of duty;' then raising his voice to call to his boys, 'Jamesu, give Mister Jacob a shilling from the household bag; you can put it down as nuts.'

He rode away with a polite wave of the hand. Jacob turned towards the group of servants and court followers with a delighted grin of triumph. 'You see,' he cried, swaggering before them, 'that's the way to do it. I frightened him. I always handle the judgies like that. You can do what you like with them.'

They gazed at him, even Jamesu, with awe and admiration.

19 Tanawe had barely run out of the house towards Akoko before Yemaja ran in from the other end to say that Ajala and his men were coming back. As she was speaking, Ajala stooped at the door. Yemaja flew at him and scratched his face, screaming that he was a thief and that she had nothing to steal. But he knocked her down with a blow in the face. The mob poured in and rifled the house in a moment. They pulled down the roofs, broke all the doors, mats, pots, stole everything valuable.

Marimi and Yemaja, her nose running with blood, continued to scream abuse and threats. They would complain to Musa, the judge, they would have Ajala flogged and put in prison. But they knew that complaints were no good. Nothing could give them back what was lost, and if they complained at all they would probably be murdered. They were screaming out of hatred and despair. Old Makunde who had been running here and there trying to rescue some of his property implored his womenfolk to be quiet.

'Be silent, you fools, you'll bring more trouble.'

But they were too angry to listen to him. They cursed him also for being a coward and an old fool.

'What are you doing, you old rotten sheep?' Marimi screamed at him, and Yemaja went into shrieks of derisive laughter. 'See our man, what a bold one!'

Yemaja was astonished by these misfortunes. She was hardly able to believe in them. She had never before seen anything like this; a crowd tearing her things to pieces. She rushed wildly about; after every curse she gazed about her with those changing looks of amazement and fear which can be seen in the eyes of a frightened calf in the butcher's hands.

Suddenly a baby was heard crying from the yard. Ajala and half a dozen more rushed to the place, pulled off the mats and earth and discovered Abba, Aissa and Makoto cowering in the deep narrow ditch. They dragged them out. Makunde and the two women were tied up, but as the women continued to scream and threaten the mob lost patience and beat them all to death.

Aissa and Makoto were not killed at once on account of the usual dispute between their captors. Ajala wanted to burn Aissa and Abba and give Makoto two hundred lashes, but Ladile's party shouted, 'Like Salente, like Salente.'

Salente was a man found guilty two years before of witchcraft. He had killed several people with the cough (influenza) and was sentenced to death. They had broken his legs and arms and left him on an ant's heap. In this way the vengeance of his spirit had been diverted upon the ants.

The dispute went on for a long time since neither Ajala nor Ladile would give way in the presence of his followers. But someone ran to fetch Obasa, and at the sight of this great man approaching all became silent.

Obasa was the most respected and the richest man in the district. He was a favourite of Bradgate, who knew him to be fearless in honesty and who had begged him to be District Head of Kolu. But he would not serve under a Mahomedan or have any dealings with such as the Waziri and Mallam Illo, the Emir's secretary, whom he looked upon as time servers and rascals.

Obasa was a tall man about fifty years old, jet black, with a handsome and intelligent face. His expression was always sad, because it seemed to him like other aristocrats of Yanrin that his country was going to the dogs.

Obasa at once took his usual place as leader because it was obvious that he knew what ought to be done and how to do it. He was experienced in procedure.

'What have these people done?' he asked.

Ajala explained how Oke had been insulted, Owule and Moshalo wounded, how Aissa had changed herself into a bitch; 'and the child is a born witch, for he was born feet foremost.'

'It's a lie,' Aissa screamed. She was still holding Abba in her arms. 'They lie. He was born like any other. He's not a witch. I didn't change.'

She threw herself on her knees towards Obasa, imploring him: 'Curse me if I lie, lord. Kill me if I don't say truth. It isn't a witch, it never was. It was sick small small, and then that bawd Fanta said it was a witch. Lord, I swear, listen only a moment.'

Her screams and protestations drowned all other voices until one of the bystanders, a public-spirited young woman, shocked to hear her interrupt a great man in this rude way, stooped and punched her in the mouth, crying, 'Be silent, beast, have you no manners?'

'Who saw her change?' Obasa asked.

Half a dozen witnesses pressed forward. An old woman, who had first noticed the yellow bitch, swore that Aissa had changed before her eyes, and caught up Abba in her teeth to gallop away with him. This evidence had great weight with Obasa, who had experience of legal enquiries and could tell when a witness was truthful and honest. But it was obvious to all that this old woman, known for her old-fashioned uprightness and integrity, was speaking the truth.

The old lady for her part had no shadow of doubt that she had seen Aissa change because she knew already that the girl was a witch and able to change herself. As for her carrying off Abba in her teeth, was it not obvious that she must have done so for how else could a dog carry a child?

'And the man,' Obasa asked, 'what has he done?'

'He struck the priestess Moshalo.'

'You wish him flogged.'

'Yes, lord.'

'But to burn the woman with her child?'

'Yes, lord.'

'Why make this difference since both have insulted Oke?'

'Lord, the woman is also a witch.'

'Don't you know then that all the Christians are witches? They worship a demon called Isa and drink his blood to give them power over spirits.'

Makoto was lying at full length with the calm face of a man resting. He could do nothing for himself and therefore he was not troubling about his fate. But Aissa after her usual manner which had made her the butt of the place could not resign herself to anything. She was too obstinate to perceive like other people that injustice is in the nature of things like bad weather and cannot be altered by resentment. She struggled wildly with the two men who held her down with their broad feet.

'Lord, lord,' she screamed, 'it's lies, it's lies, I'm not a witch. I never changed. How could I change? I don't know how. Hear me—I swear——'

Someone thrust a handful of cloth against her mouth and Obasa continued in his calm sad voice: 'And these Christian witches are the most dangerous kind because they set people by the ears, son against father and husband against wife. They want to steal our country from us and drive away our gods. Therefore they all deserve the punishment of Salente. Fetch me a pestle.'

An eager small boy intelligent and enterprising beyond his years was the first to wriggle his way through the press and bring back a pestle. His face when he lifted the heavy wooden club showed his pride and joy in doing a public and worthy service.

86

Aissa seeing the pestle began to fight like a lunatic. She screamed continuously: 'It's a lie, a lie, all lies. Believe me.'

She grasped the howling Abba so tightly that they could not prise him out of her arms. Her knees jumping up and down like the cranks of an engine made the two men who were trying to stretch out her legs stagger to and fro. She shrieked for help: 'Jesus, Jesus, come quick.'

It seemed to her incredible that she should be punished for no fault, and she fought with the desperation of hope. It could not happen, she would prevent it. Her wild struggles did in fact cause Obasa to wait until he could be sure of his aim; and even when with a dexterous swing he had broken her right ankle she continued to kick with both legs and cry out: 'Jesus, Jesus, I love you, come quick. Come quick.'

Before Obasa could change his grip for a blow from the other side his name was called by several voices and three horsemen came cantering from the Yanrin road, making the crowd scatter. They were seen to be Ali, a boy of sixteen, son of the Waziri; a mounted guardsman Suli in attendance on him, and Mallam Illo the Emir's secretary.

Ali who had lately returned from the government school at Berua was assistant treasurer, and the guardsman carried under his right arm the new ledger in which it was his master's duty to keep the Native Treasury accounts. The Treasurer Maaji Adamu was one of the old school, who could not write without blots or add up pounds, shillings and pence except upon his fingers and toes with a stick for each twenty shillings and a stone for each ten pounds.

Ali was an ugly boy, very black, with a broad flat nose full of holes from small-pox. He was dressed in an old blue turban washed white at the folds and a dirty cotton gown. His horse was a glandered screw, the worst in the royal stable, and his reins were made of string.

Although Ali was the only son of the Prime Minister of

Yanrin, he was not considered an important person because none respected his father. Waziri had been a slave and he was still regarded as the Emir's chief slave, a servant who did what his master told him. But though people thought nothing of Ali, it appeared now that he thought a good deal of himself.

Having pulled in his wretched horse from the gallop so that the beast appeared ready to fall to pieces, he sat still with a haughty air until Suli, who was incommoded by the ledger, had jumped down and taken his stirrup.

Mallam Illo was meanwhile protesting loudly over the people's heads that this affair was none of their business: 'You're a treasurer, not a dogarai, and it's very dangerous to interfere with these pagans on a feast day when half of them are drunk.'

All heard the mallam who intended to be heard, but Ali did not deign even to answer him. Having dismounted he tossed his rags over his shoulder like an Emir arranging the royal gown and strutted up to Obasa.

'What are you doing?'

'This woman is a witch.'

'Has she been tried by a court?'

Obasa, smiling as he looked down on the boy, answered carelessly, 'No, I have tried her.'

'But have you power to try cases?'

'She is guilty, I tell you, ask anybody here.'

Ajala more impatient than his master exclaimed that Aissa was a leader of the Christians who had insulted Oke and Ifa, and thus had caused them to hold back the rain.

Ali having listened with a grave and patient expression copied from that of a judge answered haughtily in his shrill voice, which could be heard far off, that all this talk was stupid. Witches had no power over rain which fell from clouds when they were made cold, and besides all knew very well that it was a wrong thing to condemn anybody without a proper trial before judges.

88

20 Umaru and the rest had managed while Aissa drew the pursuit to keep together and withdraw to Musa's house, where he had given them shelter, and now hearing that some judge had come to hear complaints against the pagans they flew to bring them. For all of them except Ojo knew themselves guilty of shedding blood. Umaru with his sword, the rest with knives, had stabbed right and left.

Makoto too, jumping up, towering over Ali, showed cuts and bruises and demanded justice; Shangoedi, having displayed a torn cheek and closed eye, fell and embraced his feet shouting at her loudest: 'Great Ali, friend of the Emir of Kano, friend of Jesus, friend of the poor, God bless you, God keep you. Lord, our master, our father and mother, save us from the wicked pagans.'

She kissed Ali's feet, weeping loudly; she was overwhelmed by his goodness and condescension. Ali who knew her for a village idiot, paid no attention to her, but pointing to Aissa, he said to Musa's constable Salko, 'Take her and the child to your master's house and let him see to her wounds.'

The crowd subdued already by his confident authority eagerly helped Salko to carry Aissa away, and could be heard urging each other to be careful of her: 'Didn't you hear what his lordship told you, you clumsy fool.'

Ali pointing to Obasa said to Suli, 'Tie this man up.'

Constable Suli, who in his turban overtopped all others, handed the horses' bridles to a bystander and took Obasa by the arm.

Obasa astounded by this indignity could not utter a word and made no motion to protect himself, but Ajala rushed to his help. Makoto caught hold of Ajala and the pair wrestled furiously. Half a dozen pagans on one side and the little group

89

of Christians on the other flew at each other and Ali was hustled aside.

Mallam Illo, who had not dismounted from his horse, shouted: 'Come now—enough—hurry up—run for it.'

But Ali, enraged by this momentary loss of dignity, darted at the fighters, crying in shrill tones, 'How dare you behave like this, you blackguards, in the presence of the court. Tie these men up, Suli.'

Suli had not been able to tie up Obasa because he was impeded by the ledger, which he could not put down; but now he thrust it into Obasa's left hand, saying, 'Take care of that,' and then quickly tied up his right hand to his neck. Meanwhile he glared at Makoto and Ladile and threatened them: 'Rascals, blackguards, you'll catch it yet.'

He spoke to them angrily because he was afraid of their walking off before he could tie them, but they did not do so; they stood like schoolboys about to be punished, making faces expressive of their sense of injustice, but not daring to say a word aloud.

The crowd listened to Mallam Illo, who was protesting loudly against these arrests, but especially that of Obasa. Mallam Illo never lost an opportunity of doing the popular thing because as the Emir's secretary and a tax collector he was a hated man.

He had no wish to change Ali's mind, because he did not want to be responsible for the consequences of a riot; but he was confident that the boy would not change his mind on account of a protest given before witnesses, and in this he was right.

Ali answered haughtily, 'It doesn't matter who he is. He was doing a wrong thing, and therefore he must be taken up.' Then seeing that the people were attentive and anxious like other boys to teach them what was the proper thing as he had learnt it at school, he raised his voice and addressed them: 'Is not the law the same for all men? That is justice, and justice is most excellent. When I was at Berua school, the great white man, the resident, came to us and said, "This football is a game, but it is a game like the life of man." '

Ali turned towards the people, waved his hands, became excited and nervous and began to lose his dignity, but just when he was going to enlarge on this very important matter of what the great white man had said, a thing that it was most necessary for everybody to know, Shangoedi who had just become aware of Makoto's arrest, flew to his rescue.

Shangoedi saw now that Ali was not a friend of Jesus, but a cunning hypocrite who had pretended to help the Christians in order to betray them. She wanted to tear his eyes out. She was breathless with rage. 'Look at him,' she shrieked, fighting her way through the crowd, 'the dirty little by-blow. The traitor, the liar. The son of a hole. He thinks he's a chief and he's only a bastard. Jesus curse him.' Bursting through the people she flew at the boy and shrieked her curses in his face. Suli holding three prisoners could not assist his master, and Mallam Illo turned his horse's head. Ali scorning to fly from the angry woman stood where he was and did not even look at her. He tried to ignore the rude foolish creature; but his position was dangerous and unpleasant, and the crowd perceiving it, and not being individually responsible, began to laugh and watched with malicious interest.

Suli at last clinching the knot on Makoto's neck made a motion to seize Shangoedi, but Ali with a grand gesture said, 'No, let her alone—it doesn't matter.' Then seeing that this was his chance to make a good exit, he walked to his horse. Shangoedi enraged by his contempt ran after him, screaming: 'Traitor, enemy of Jesus—may God wither you,' and seeing him about to mount she clawed at his face and tore his gown.

Suli raised his spear-butt to drive it into the woman's face, but Ali said again sharply, 'Let her alone—she doesn't understand anything.'

21 Ali with his prisoners met Bradgate on the road a mile out from Akoko. Bradgate was delighted with the boy's pluck and good sense, and though he told him that he would have done better to take Obasa's name and order him to come up for judgment, than to drag him through the country at the end of a rope, he was careful to make the reproof light and the praise strong. He put him in charge of the prisoners until their witnesses could arrive, and this post of responsibility was the highest reward he could have offered the boy, who could not hide his joy and pride in it.

After Bradgate's departure the next morning to answer the mail at Yanrin, he spread his sleeping mat on the residency verandah and walked about the camp all day with his lips cocked up as if he were the master of it all. He was hard put to it to fill his time with appropriate duties. But sometimes he went to the river and examined it attentively as Bradgate had done, stooping down, aiming through a hole in his thumb and fingers, shaking his head and saying impatiently to the by-standers, two village children, or an old woman dressed in a bunch of leaves and a sharp stick thrust out between her buttocks like a tail: 'That's a bad place there, I shall have to take care of that place when we build the bridge,' and frequently bringing out a sheet of official foolscap, he would squat in the compound, at a place open to view from all sides, and shout out to a noisy small boy or passer-by, 'Be silent there.' Then he could be seen moving his lips, jerking his pen, frowning in his difficult calculations, of how many times five pounds one and ninepence could be divided by fourteen and threepence, or what was the annual amount of fourpence halfpenny a week. These were sums remembered from his last term at school. He did not think of devising new ones.

Every half hour he would walk into the prisoners' hut and ask them in a kind voice: 'Do you want to see me about anything? Have you any complaints?'

These were the questions Bradgate asked of prisoners, and Ali knew they were the proper thing. He even copied Bradgate's voice.

When Ali went to the village he took care to put on his best gown, his boots and his sword, and to swagger with his grandest air, because his road took him past the quarters of the court and the council chamber.

Bradgate had commanded the Emir and court to stay in Akoko till the bridge was made; and the Haji had summoned his best builders to make huts for them.

A large flat-topped hut twenty foot square, of bright new yellow mats glittering like metal, was planted by the road for the Emir's headquarters; and here he sat all day with one councillor or another, gazing at his hands folded in his lap or breathing out a text like a sigh. In each wall of the house there was a big square door, ten feet wide, so that to the passer-by outside the councillors appeared like triangular white sacks tied up with black rope and stooked together in the middle shadow of the roof; while to the councillors within the whole land of Yanrin could be seen in four square pictures; to the north all black bush up to the white sky; to the west, old yam fields, tall jungle, and the Niger like an ocean; to the south, the rest camp and the big baobab; to the east, the deep gully of the Akoko river curling upwards into the right hand corner, with a lace-work of bright pools in its muddy bottom and one long crooked pole stuck in the middle of it and gradually falling over. This pole represented all the bridge construction accomplished since Bradgate's going, and he had been promised the whole completed on his return in six days. But the council were not yet troubled about their contract. They did not even look towards the river. They were still enjoying the relief of Bradgate's departure.

What luxury to sit in the shade and know that he was far away; that from morning to night there would be nothing to do.

The Emir, the old Alkali, Mallam Isa, quiet and pious Mahomedans, murmured gently together by the hour.

'Do you remember Nagwomachi (a great slave raiding chief of Kontagora) and what he did in Yanrin?'

'Not a man, a woman or child left in the whole town. Not a horse or a goat.'

'Ah, that was a man.'

'Nagwomachi had a roan horse that could jump the Akoko.'

'That's a very good kind of horse, a roan.'

'Ah! I always like a roan with five white points. But let him have a long neck.'

'Thick too. Let his neck be thick.'

'I had a horse like that myself in the year before Big Medals (Lugard) went to Bussa. It cost me four pounds from a Katsina man. Now one day when I was riding this Katsina roan to Kontagora in a time of peace, Nagwomachi sent for me and said:

'He sent his Madaiki, I suppose. The Nupe with a dead hand.'

'Pardon, Alkali, Madaikin Sarkin Sudan was not a Nupe. He was a Fulah; he was killed by the duck gun (mountain gun) in the white man's war, he was reputed to be a changer, and I believe it, for his eyes were like a hyena's.'

'Yes, he was a changer, but Nagwomachi also knew witch-craft. He could see through walls.'

'What, now that surprises me. Yes, your honour, I'm surprised. I never heard that before.'

22 When Ali passed the door, swaggering with his arms as if, as they say, his back was itching, this murmured talk of the old gentlemen ceased and they gazed at the boy with wonder and perplexity. Whence did the son of a slave, not sixteen years old, ugly, friendless, poor, derive such reckless self-confidence, such rash energy.

The Emir sighed; Mallam Adamu's eyes bulged with stupe-faction at his understrapper; the old Alkali looked under his lids with a pondering air.

These, the oldest and the wisest of the council, the Emir's friends, did not rage against Ali; they regarded him as one other unpleasant product of the new régime; they looked at him with distaste and surprise.

Yerima on the other hand hated Ali. When Yerima came to council there was no peace. The little pagan had no manners, no decorum. He screamed, cursed, the foam spattered from his mouth. He was contemptible but unluckily he did not care.

Yerima would rush into the chamber in his loin cloth and wearing only a cap on his head. He would bawl for hours his hatred against Bradgate, the white men, the Yorubas, all strangers, all new things and the bridge. Peace and comfort vanished before him.

Everything is getting worse, he would shout at them: 'The clerks come, Yorubas, white men, these Christians now. All is being spoilt. You do nothing, you cowards. Soon the railway will come. Berua got it and look at Berua. The old judge said, make this railway, and all the Yoruba thieves and whores and soldier's women, all the corrupt boys and Christians in the land came there and spoilt it. See Berua now. The young men push you into the drain, the girls laugh in your beard, the people are like shameless animals. No railway, I say, no bridge—no roads, these are very bad things. Children must not go to school to learn to spit upon their mothers and fathers. We'll stop these Christians and their witchcraft.'

Yerima wanted to burn Aissa for a witch and cut Ali's throat so that he should not witness against Obasa. He could hardly be prevented from rushing out on the boy with his sword. But Mallam Illo and the Alkali restrained him. They pointed out that Ali was in favour with Bradgate. It would be risky even to threaten him: 'but you have only to wait.' They soothed the furious old man: 'The judge will go away soon and then you can punish him as you choose.'

23 Salko and his followers had carried Aissa to the nearest house, but as soon as Ali went away she was taken to the lock-up. Umaru also who scorned to obey Musa when he was ordered to leave the town, was arrested.

It is usual in Nigeria for one who has been punished to thank his judges and executioners and ask their pardon, like the dog who licks his master's boots while he is being flogged; but Aissa was too excited and impatient to behave herself properly like other people or even to consider how she ought to behave. She fought with her gaolers and abused and threatened everyone who came near her.

'You touch me,' she screamed, 'and Jesus will curse you; you touch Abba and fire will burn you up.'

Even when the child was brought to her in order to keep her quiet (for as old Musa pointed out, it could be taken away again as soon as the council decided what to do with the mother), she refused to be pacified, but shrieked out curses at anybody who should harm Gajere in a voice that could be heard over half the quarter. Fear and anger gave her such power that even Musa could feel it and went about in a state of fuss, without his turban, saying that the woman was a dangerous one, the worst he had ever known. But when, exasperated, he threatened her with the whip, she only screamed the louder, calling upon Jesus, Ojo, Mister Carr, Umaru and the Holy Spirit, to avenge her.

Umaru who at his own request had been placed at the far end of the room as far as possible from Aissa, now came to Musa's help and told her to be quiet.

'Let them send me back to Shibi, then,' she screamed, 'and my man too, before God comes to burn them up with the drought and starve them all, the dogs.'

'You flatter yourself,' said the Fulani with his usual austerity, 'God doesn't concern himself with blackguards and loose women.'

'It's a lie,' Aissa bawled; 'I'm as good as anybody and a good deal better than you are, you gaolbird.'

'You left us there in the market place and went back to your fornication. You thought you would cheat God like that. But the Bible says that you can't make a fool of God.'

At this Aissa, who had given everybody hope of a little peace, began to make more noise than ever, only now she cursed Umaru as well as Musa and the Kolua.

She was more violent against Umaru because she felt that there was something in what he said. She did not take the trouble to recall her recent conduct, but she now had a sensation as if parts of it were sinful. For this reason she not only abused Umaru but sought to make up to God also.

'You are very good to me, God,' she told him: 'I belong to you now. I you girl, I good Christian girl. Abba, Gajere, belong for you too. Abba good Christian chile. Gajere want to be Christian too much. He agree for you God, I tink you fit agree for him. He very good man, Gajere.'

She did not humble herself before God because she did not wish to appear like one with a guilty conscience; and she spoke to Jesus in the same manner. 'Jesus you do plenty good thing for me I always do good for you, pray you every day, Jesus. You good frien to me Jesus, I know that.'

But she knew that she had sinned against them and on the next night when her leg had begun to swell and throb and her whole body was burning with fever, she felt someone looking at her. She turned round, and there through a chink at the edge of the roof a stern eye like a star was fixed upon her. She sprang aside with a loud scream and the eye was gone. But something moved towards her in the darkness. A cold air breathed on her face. Fearful that the spirit would enter her she caught herself by the nose, and kept her mouth shut. This stratagem, always recommended in the district to exclude spirits, was successful, but naturally it still further irritated the messenger of God, who said to her at once in an angry voice, 'You very wicked girl, Aissa.'

'I do nutting, I do nutting,' Aissa screamed, forgetting her precautions in order to defend her character. But she knew that she had committed very bad sins, in leaving the mission, in getting drunk, in lying with Gajere who was several other women's husband.

'You fool girl, Aissa,' said the spirit; 'you say you no run away, you no leave Ma Carr, you no drink dem beer.'

'Oh, sah, I no want drink dem beer, I no like dem beer, he make me sick for belly.'

'You wicked girl what you tell me? You no tink God no see you go wit dat pagan man. You tink you put cloth over your head, God no see. You no tink, you fool girl, he send his eyes look under cloth, see you play with Gajere?'

'No, no, no,' Aissa screamed in terror, holding Abba beneath her so tightly that he also began to howl, 'I no love him, sah. I no love him tall.'

'What!' cried the spirit, growing more and more angry; 'you go tell me lie like dat? What you tink God go do to you for dat? You no fraid go to hell den one time? You no fear dem fire, he burn you? You go to hell, Aissa, what you do for Abba? He go stay here for people, dey tie him for bush—de kuras (hyenas) eat him. Ha, you didn't tink of dat.'

But Aissa had thought of this. Every native woman, sick or in danger, thinks of it, because she knows that if she dies the baby will probably die too. This is why a native woman with a child at the breast will make a better fight for her life, so long as she cares for the child, than the stoutest-hearted man. Aissa screamed breathlessly that she did not love Gajere. 'What,' she cried, 'you tink I lak dat ugly pagan man, Gajere—no woman fit lak dat rubbish.'

The spirit was not deceived and Aissa scarcely hoped to deceive it, but she continued to argue without ceasing. Sometimes she shrieked with anger at the charges brought against her, sometimes she begged for mercy, sometimes she laughed at the very notion of having anything to do with such a person as Gajere.

These shouts and cries terrified Kolu, already much disturbed by the escape of Umaru (an old escaper), who had simply vanished out of the prison into the air, leaving his irons on the ground. The people threatened to burn the hut over the witch and her demon baby; and Musa knowing that he would be held responsible for them by the council determined to get rid of them at once. Abba was handed over to Owule, who claimed the child as a witch and undertook to answer for it, and Aissa was sent to Yanrin prison.

24 Yanrin Prison stands in the centre of the town on one side of the square market place, whose others are filled with the Emir's palace, the Treasury, court house and mosque, and on the fourth, the town houses of certain great nobles, feudal chiefs of the sub-districts.

All these buildings are of yellow mud; their high walls sloping back like those of a fortress have few and small windows. The roofs are flat and surrounded by ramparts, with machicolations from which, like immensely long gun barrels aimed at the square below, project spouts of palm wood.

The ground of the square is not flat. The palace and the prison stand on mountains formed by the ruins of former palaces and prisons built on the same site for hundreds of years. The courthouse is in a deep hole, a marsh in the wet season, and the Treasury, a high square tower, clings to a flank of the palace mound.

To the north the ground falls quickly away and gathers into a deep road like the bed of a stream, which in a dozen curves at last reaches the main gate.

The prison had lately been repaired and cleaned by a new chief of police, Zeggi. Zeggi was an old veteran of many wars. He had fought for the Mahdi at Omdurman and the French against Rabeh; against the English at Sakoto in 1906, and for the Germans as a sergeant, in 1915. He had finished this last war, after being wounded and left for dead, as a British headman of carriers; and came to Yanrin with recommendations which secured the favour both of the native authorities and Bradgate. The Emir approved him because he could shoot and because he was likely to be faithful; Bradgate because he had the training of a soldier and understood the nature of discipline from both ends, the commanding and the commanded.

The old man was a half bred Bauchi pagan about sixty years old and under five foot high. His frame was that of a sickly small boy, his bow legs were as fragile as a bird's, and his jumper, blowing about, seemed to hang on the ribs of a little basket. His face had tumbled in so that it appeared like that of a dried head picked up on some battlefield, and his little red eyes blinked at the bottom of deep round holes. He had three teeth, two above, and one below. Zeggi's body was old and ruined, worn out by debauchery and hardships, but he seemed to be quite unaware of this fact. Probably he had never seen himself in a looking glass. He swaggered about Yanrin, an old military fez cocked over one eye, with the lively gait and cheerful self-satisfaction of a corporal lady killer. His ridiculous legs twinkled about the town and the station from morning till night. He was ready for anything or anybody. It was Zeggi who was sent to Bradgate with bad news because he was not afraid to deliver it. He was even pleased with such an errand, because it gave him the chance of displaying before Bradgate who understood such things the smartness of his salute. He would march into the office, right turn, salute like a guardsman, his hand quivering with zeal, and shout in a loud cracked voice: 'Lion, Lord! the Lord of Yanrin, my master, gives you a thousand salutations. Also all the tax money which you sent to Berua has fallen into the river.' He would watch Bradgate's anger, answer all his questions with the same dutiful promptness and clarity, take his orders, salute again, right turn, and go into barracks for a chat and a drink with the police.

When Aissa the witch, with her putrefying leg, arguing ceaselessly with unseen spirits, was put into Yanrin gaol, everyone including Zeggi was disgusted and alarmed. But Zeggi did not say so because he considered it unbefitting to him as a man in authority to show such feelings. All including Zeggi were fearful of going near Aissa in case she should turn

101

herself into a dog or a leopard and tear them to pieces; but for Zeggi with his training and his self-respect founded on that training it was impossible to admit even to himself that he was afraid. He swallowed half a glass of gin, hung all his charms round his neck and his war medal on his breast, and marched into the cell. But Aissa paid no attention to him. She was in high fever, laughing and chattering to a bundle of rags which had been given to her in exchange for Abba.

Zeggi saw that the woman was very ill, but he knew his duty because it was written down for him. He could not read, but he could point to the clause which laid down his responsibility for the health and welfare of his prisoners.

Zeggi was proud of his gaol and proud also of understanding the proper way to do things—that is, the white soldier's way. An order meant something quite different to him than to the rest of his colleagues in the native administration. He had grasped the notions of duty and obedience, of routine, and even the idea of them. He knew why they were valuable, and like other simple men who have acquired by chance or instruction some fragment of systematic knowledge, he set the highest value on it. It was his religion, his touchstone, his glory. He loved to talk about it, to shout at some rustic just drafted into the guard: 'Don't you know what an order is. Ah—you dog eater, you bumpkin. What would happen if no one obeyed orders. Why, don't you see, you fool, that everything would go to the devil. But it's easy to perceive that you've never been a white man's soldier. How could you know anything, you yam-headed son of a hoe.'

Zeggi briskly set about his official duty of curing Aissa. He sent at once for the best doctor in the place, who tied a rope round her leg to prevent the bad influence ascending further into her body and poured cold water over her head to cure the fever. At the same time he contradicted Zeggi's diagnosis of possession by the spirit of Jesus.

Unlearned people, this Mallam explained, were accustomed to say that Christian witches were possessed by Isa to whom they owed their surprising impudence and conceit, but in fact Isa was not a spirit but a prophet, like Ibrahim, Musa and Adamu (Abraham, Moses and Adam). This woman was possessed by some evil spirit, and not Isa whom all good Mahomedans revere.

When Aissa did not improve, Zeggi was in and out of the cell twenty times a day. He gave her quinine from his own private store purchased from Bradgate's servants at a penny a tablet, and poured more buckets of water on her head. Nevertheless she grew worse. Sometimes she chattered like a monkey, laughed and flirted; then she would cry for Abba and Gajere and utter shrieks that could be heard in the market so that the crowds stood outside open-mouthed, staring at the high wall and saying to each other: 'It's the Christian witch who struck Owule, she's cursing Zeggi now. Better him than us.'

They were pleased to think that Zeggi was in danger because they were jealous of all persons in authority; and this though they themselves would not have taken any post of responsibility. A song about Zeggi was instantly popular because it sprang from the popular feeling and expressed it.

> 'Zeggi is sick,
> His bowels wither.
> What do you fear, Zeggi?
> A girl with one leg.
> Zeggi is sick.
> She has cursed him.
> Zeggi is afraid
> She'll change one day
> And tear your guts, Zeggi.'

Zeggi paid no attention to the people and their ways. He never noticed what others were thinking. He was too busy. He was seen marching about the prison and the town all day, with his French quick step, and his fez over his eyebrow, seeking anybody who had treated a case like Aissa's. Finally a mallam from Sokoto gave it as his opinion that since Aissa was a Christian her illness would only surrender to a Christian medicine; for, said he, 'Disease is a demon and demons only understand their own language.'

It happened luckily that a Yoruba kola-nut trader, an old man called Clarence Adebu, was lodging in the zungo, or public hostel. Adebu was well known to possess a Bible for he sold charms from it even in Yanrin; and also Isa's blood in small scent bottles.

When Zeggi applied to him he came at once to see Aissa, and having looked at her leg, he put on his spectacles and read from the Bible in Yoruba: 'If your leg troubles you, cut it off; if your eye, take it out.'

He wrote these words on a board and also on a piece of King's paper—that is to say, a piece of paper from Bradgate's office stamped with the royal arms. Such paper, which could be found in the waste paper basket, had a good sale in the market because of its power as medicine. Zeggi and he then cut off Aissa's leg at the ankle and cauterized the stump with a hot knife. They bound the paper to the wound in a plaster of chewed tobacco leaves. Then having washed the ink of the magic words from the board into a calabash of water they poured the mixture down the patient's throat. She mended at once. The swelling of the leg decreased, the fever left her. When Zeggi assured her on his honour that Gajere and Abba were at the mission she became cheerful and hungry, asked for food and tried to flirt with the warders, shouting jokes at them which would have been thought very good from anybody but a witch.

25 This improvement gave great pleasure to Zeggi, who pointed out to friends like Sergeant Momo Sokoto of Bradgate's detachment how much harder it was to cure a witch of two or three devils at the same time than an ordinary criminal of one. Zeggi, in fact, who had had no opportunity of distinguishing himself for a long time past, was rejuvenated by this success. When the Sergeant, a man of authority and sparing of words, praised him, he could not hide his delight. His characteristic quickstep through town and barracks became a kind of prance, his monkey-face was wrinkled all over with irrepressible smiles, his little eyes were screwed up as if someone were tickling him, his fez was stuck to his left eyebrow at such an angle that it appeared like a defiance to natural law as well as the town mob.

The only flaw in the man's perfect happiness (and Zeggi was old and worn-out) was the absence of Bradgate, the Emir and the court, his masters who would know how to appreciate his courage and reliability. But he expected them every day, and meanwhile used the time profitably by stuffing Aissa with food and oiling her skin till she glistened like a bride.

Instead however of receiving due praise for his feat, Zeggi was set a harder one—the council sent him an urgent command to get rid of the woman at once.

Waziri himself brought the order. Waziri who had till two days before been engaged upon the dangerous and thankless task of collecting the Emir's illegal land taxes on the northern frontier had now been recalled post-haste to extricate his master from his difficulties. His orders were to soothe Bradgate, build the bridge, arrange the trial so that Obasa should escape imprisonment, placate Yerima and correct his son Ali. He was to do these things at once on pain of discharge, that is to say, of the complete ruin of himself and his family.

These terms may seem hard but neither master nor slave found them anything but reasonable, and they had the desired effect of producing extraordinary efforts in the latter. He scarcely left the saddle in three days. By the time he arrived in Yanrin he had ridden two hundred miles in quest of timber, workmen, witnesses, carrying threats and bribes over half the country; he was in such a condition of weariness and dirt that even the people in the street, accustomed to see him tired and dirty, exclaimed to each other and made jokes about him and his friend Zeggi greeted him with polite cries of sympathy.

But the old man did not pity himself. He was too much preoccupied and too angry with Ali. He wept while he related the boy's ruinous folly. 'But what could I have done?' he lamented, wringing his twisted fingers. 'I did not want him to go to the white man's school. It was the judge who said that he must go and learn like a judge. But what do the white men know about our work. If it wasn't for you and me this Kolu rubbish would soon destroy everything. But Bradgy insisted and now the boy is done for. They've filled him with their white man's nonsense and he is simply a fool, a conceited bighead who thinks he knows better than the oldest and most experienced men in the whole country. And you can't make him change, he's as obstinate as a hillman. And now they'll cut him to pieces. Yerima will poison him—he's only waiting till the judge goes to Berua. They'll serve him like Musa, and who can blame them?'

Musa was an assistant court clerk who had reported to Bradgate, about a year before, a pagan elder for bribery—he had died soon afterwards in such agony that rumours of it came to Bradgate even though he had been on leave at the time. But it had been proved to him by Musa's own family

106

with the greatest eagerness that the boy had died of a strong fever.

Zeggi was greatly moved by the piteous anxiety and grief of his old friend, and frequently interrupted his lamentations with cries of sympathy like, 'Allah,' and 'God have mercy on us,' which the occasion and his own feelings demanded.

'As for the woman,' he assured him warmly, 'you needn't worry about her. I'll settle that business for you in a minute.'

'Yes, but nothing must be known; remember that Bradgy is here now. It isn't as if he was at his own country.'

'That's all right, friend; I know a place where the hyenas will finish off even her bones in a single hour. And I'll knock her on the head myself. I hope you can depend on Zeggi by this time.'

26 The first scheme did not prove satisfactory because Zeggi was not strong enough to tie and carry Aissa by himself, and none of the police would assist him. They feared Aissa's revenge. They pointed out that the last witch put to death in Yanrin, a girl of fifteen called Esu, had caused her two executioners to be found out by Bradgate and sent to prison in Kaduna, where both had died.

Luckily Aissa herself suggested a way out of the difficulty by asking when she was to go back to Shibi.

Zeggi saw at once that if Aissa departed willingly her ill will need not be feared and strong men would not be required to carry her through the town and the bush. He therefore answered her: 'On the first dark night—for if the Kolua catch you, they will kill you.'

Then delighted with his new plan the little soldier went off to the house of Kokode, a midwife and also a professional witch killer. Kokode would undertake the charge of any witch child, that is to say, a twin, one born with teeth, or feet foremost, or with any suspicious deformity proclaiming it's difference from respectable babies, and get rid of it either by burying it alive or drowning, for a fee of five shillings upwards.

Even Kokode was afraid of Aissa, whose reputation in Yanrin grew every day, but Zeggi by a mixture of flattery and threats, a bribe of five shillings and a bottle of gin persuaded her at last to lend her assistance.

Two nights later, at three in the morning, Zeggi and Kokode brought Aissa out of prison through the back door of Zeggi's own house and Kokode bore her on her back to a thicket near Ketemfe, a place avoided by everybody on account of its ghosts, leopards, hyenas. Aissa, to whom Zeggi had given a pint of the best beer, was in the highest spirits, and now that she found herself so near the river and far from her pagan enemies in Kolu and Yanrin, she began to sing, not hymns, but a lively ballad about a former chief of Yanrin, renowned for gallantry. Zeggi joined in the song and at the same time gave Kokode the signal by a poke in the back. Kokode dropped the girl and threw a rope round her neck. Aissa said in a tone of surprise, 'Look out, old girl, you've got my head caught.'

There was no moon, but the stars gave a little light, so that solid objects appeared slightly blacker than the air. Aissa could be seen like a round bundle. Zeggi aimed a blow at her with his matchet, when suddenly the bundle became an oblong; Aissa stretched herself out on all fours and darted at Zeggi's legs like a wild pig.

Zeggi and Kokode ran off in opposite directions, but the pig chased Zeggi for a mile, coming so close to him that he felt its hot breath on his legs. Luckily he had bought the day before a new charm against changers, and so at last by throwing himself into a hole near the Ketemfe road he escaped with his life.

At dawn he returned safely home. Zeggi did not wish this story to be known because he was ashamed of running away even from a witch-pig; but his face was saved by a strange mistake of Kokode's. For Kokode, who had run to a hunter's camp, told them that it was she whom Aissa had chased in the form of a huge bird with clattering beak and fiery yellow eyes. Moreover, the men themselves blocking up their doors and windows in terror, heard the bird's great wings beating over the roof. So that in Yanrin it was believed that Aissa had escaped in the shape of a bird.

27 On the morning of Obasa's trial Waziri's confidential servant, a young Fulani with the countenance of a Pharaoh and the cunning of a rat, entered with presents of nuts and cloth to Bradgate's household and asked politely if the master had arisen in good health.

Audu understanding very well what this meant replied that the judge had not yet dressed and that he was in a very bad temper.

This was quite true. Bradgate had been greatly annoyed by the riot in Kolu, for which he held the Carrs responsible.

Bradgate was of course a loyal son of the Church, for which he had filial love and respect, but he had not been to a service for thirty years, and he had even a vague notion that this abstinence was meritorious, that on the whole he showed himself a man of religious probity in not going, because he had another vague notion that the creed, if he ever had time to examine it and find out its real meaning, would not represent his own belief, whatever it was, when he had time to look into it.

He had of course discussed religious questions with friends, laymen, but the results had only confirmed his impression that they were difficult and perhaps dangerous to peace of mind. With parsons he avoided such subjects altogether. He knew of course that the majority of them would be considerate and polite, skating lightly over his ignorance (if indeed he was ignorant) and his slackness (if he was slack, he had no time to find out) but there were exceptions. His friend Harries had been attacked by a missionary in the presence of a whole Scotch club, and the man had refused to be put off with jokes and smiles.

The Carrs of course were not that sort. But weren't they? Carr had a funny accent. And now this affair at Kolu. A sahib might have done as much, a keen man, and all honour to him, but would he have done it without warning. Was it quite cricket?

He used all his diplomatic tact in the necessary remonstrance.

Dear Carr,

I'm sorry about the Kolu row. I had no idea that you were coming into this division or I'd have warned you. It was a great relief to me when I heard that neither you nor Mrs. Carr received any damage.

What a pity that the disturbance should have happened just now, when the people were a bit restless on account of the drought, and what we particularly needed in Yanrin was peace and quiet to open the roads and develop trade. It seems impossible to do much with education or enlighten- ment for people whose average total income is under five pounds a year.

I wonder would you give some of your keener disciples a hint to lie low for the present, at least until the rains break. It would be a real disaster if anyone got badly hurt. I haven't forgotten Mrs. Carr's very kind hospitality in Shibi.

I'm sending her some English potatoes. I think a real potato now and then is as good as a bottle of tonic.

With kindest regards to you both,

Sincerely yours

A. D. Bradgate

P.S.—I remember you said something about the right of missions to settle in Yanrin. There is no such right anywhere. The mission is allowed dum bene se gesserit *only, to quote the lawyers, even in Shibi.*

Bradgate had taken some time to compose this letter and was proud of it. It seemed to him that no one could be offended by it, and yet it contained all that the case required—a statement of the situation obvious and unanswerable in its truth—a gentle reproach for endangering it—a command not to do so again, and in the postscript the threat, softened by Latin, of the possible consequences of disregarding that order.

But his worst fears had been realized. Carr had answered thus, in a letter at that moment in his hand:

Shibi,

10.4.28

Dear Mr. Bradgate,

The Kolu row, as you call it, was caused entirely by your friends the pagan priests.

My wife and I quite understand that we have no legal right to bring the knowledge of God to your people. He who first brought the message of love and hope to the world was also considered an enemy of government.

I have warned those whom you call my keener disciples that the Yanrin government does not like them, and is far from desiring the poorer people to hear the truth or know the Saviour, but some of them seem to think that there are arguments on the other side. They are, as you say, keen chaps and so hard to restrain from helping others, especially

111

*those whom they look upon as brothers and whom they see
making quite an unnecessary mess and misery of their lives,
and dying without a glimmer of hope of a better one.*

*But I will try to make them neglect their Christian duty, as
far as it conflicts with government orders, at least for the
present. Will you on your side ask your friends the pagans
to keep some of their keener disciples from throwing offal
and insults at perfectly harmless lads and women from the
mission (some of them not even Church members yet, but
merely their relations) when they dare to attend Sabongari
market. As their objects are purely commercial and selfish,
I think they are even entitled to your protection. I'm sorry
we don't see eye to eye in these matters, but I suppose it
can hardly be expected.*

*Mrs. Carr thanks you for the potatoes which are greatly
appreciated. I send you some pumpkins and tomatoes which
I hope you will like even though they were grown by one
of the keener disciples now I understand in Yanrin gaol,
threatened with imprisonment and a hundred to one chance
of death by dysentery, influenza, syphilis, etc., or some
other friend of peace and good government.*

Yours faithfully

H. J. Carr.

This letter disgusted Bradgate like a mean trick. He read
again, 'as their objects are purely commercial and selfish,' and
the words made him hot with rage. For he knew that his objects
were not purely commercial and selfish. Damn it, he had nearly
killed himself for these apes at Kolu, and what for? Who cared
or knew how hard he worked if he filled in the monthly returns,
an hour's job. The charge was the typical piece of cocksure
self-righteousness to be expected from your radical and fanatic
everywhere.

Yet it went home, because Bradgate suspected that he could

not answer the question offhand, What are you really doing in Yanrin? What are you driving at? That the religious questions might after all be of some little importance, that they might have some connection with education, for instance, which he knew to be important. He suspected but he did not know because he did not want to know. He had no time to bother about such matters just now. As soon therefore as the thought appeared in his mind or rather a little before his uneasiness was formed into a thought he turned from it and bawled for his shaving water.

But he was disgusted with Carr, and when Audu brought the water full of Akoko mud he damned him in a manner which deeply offended the boy accustomed to his usual good nature.

He flatly refused to see Waziri.

28 But Waziri was not to be put off. For Ali's sake, for his own sake, for everybody's sake he had to see Bradgate and put him in a good temper. He therefore watched for his moment, and then thrusting Audu aside, suddenly appeared in the middle of the mud floor within three yards of the district officer, who, dressed in a pair of short white drawers and red slippers, was seated on a box before two other boxes, piled one upon the other to make a dressing table.

With one cheek shaved and one still covered with soap, he glared sideways at Waziri with a very unfriendly expression and said nothing. Waziri was in fact ashamed. He had committed an act of insulting rudeness. His whole ramshackle framework of bones and dirt which had not been in bed for thirty hours trembled from head to foot with terror and weakness. But his face expressed the joy of one who meets his beloved unexpectedly after long years of waiting. His blood-ringed eyes were

113

opened to their widest, his long yellow front teeth were bared to the gums, the corners of his mouth showed black caverns behind the broken stumps of his grinders, he threw out his arms so that his gown sleeves were extended like huge wings and fell on his knees close to Bradgate's left slipper with a loud cry of delight.

'Oh Lord, oh master, what joy to see you again. That pleases the heart indeed.'

Then, before Bradgate could utter a word, he began to bob up and down, shouting in a tearful voice: 'Master, lord, I am a bad one, a worthless person. I come to repent. I repent before you, lord' (striking his forehead on the earth). 'By my badness, mine alone, your great works are hindered.' Waziri always took upon himself the faults of the native administration because this endeared him to the minister responsible, and did not deceive Bradgate, who knew that Waziri was the most dependable of them all, because the most dependent, and ambitious for his son.

Bradgate said severely: 'Yes, they've made a nice mess of things here,' but already he was softened by the knowledge that the Waziri was anxious to agree with him, to win his favour; moreover, the very sight of the man bringing new practical difficulties for solution, took his mind away from Carr and religion. He repeated, 'Yes, a nice mess,' but added at once in a friendly tone: 'I'm not blaming you for that, Waziri. It's Tafirki who isn't fit for his job. I suppose they've done nothing while I've been away.'

'Lord, the building has begun. Only come and see.'

In fact Waziri had set the whole village of Akoko, men, women and children, to cut bush and carry timber, so that when Bradgate looked out of his door he could see the work going busily forward. A group in the river bed were struggling with the first of the long poles; the women on the bank looked on. Others were clearing away the scrub, little naked children

114

of two and three only just able to walk, were trotting up and down with important looks, carrying on their heads a single faggot or an empty calabash.

All were enjoying themselves, because although the work seemed to them stupid and unnecessary it was new, and provided them with a subject for interest and conversation; the young men below were already displaying feats of strength before the girls, the clever ones their cleverness in much advice, the women as spectators joked and laughed, the children delighted in being useful.

A scene like this could not help but please Bradgate, who loved to be busy, and he exclaimed: 'So something's being done at last.'

At the time of the trial when the table and chair had been set up beneath the baobab, with the Emir seated on his carpet at one side and the Alkali without a carpet at the other; the elders, guards, and messengers behind; the witnesses and spectators, a great crowd including half the population of Kolu and many from Shibi, Yanrin, and Ketemfe, squatting in front, so closely packed that they resembled a beach of parti-coloured stones; Bradgate and Waziri were wading about in the bed of the river with sounding poles, surrounded by an admiring, arguing, advising, crowd of villagers.

Both were covered with mud, and Waziri's blue gown, tucked up to his armpits, trailed behind through the pools of slime. He could be seen bowing at every word of Bradgate's, and his voice could be heard a hundred yards away shouting: 'That's it, lord. Your wisdom has spoken. This is the place. Yes, or that one. Yes, indeed, that is a better one.'

Thus Bradgate when he came at last, after a bath, to try the case, was in a very good temper. Moreover he was in a hurry. His loads were packed and his pony saddled to keep an appointment with the D.O. of the next division, Daji, sixteen miles away. He made short work of the prisoners, gave Makoto and

Ajala a month for wounding, and ordered the arrests of Umaru, Aissa, Gajere and Ojo for assaults.

Obasa's case proved more difficult, because a dozen witnesses swore that the woman had not been hurt at all, and others that she had hurt herself in running away from the constables after her unprovoked attack on Owule. Obasa himself, being asked if he had anything to say for himself, answered: 'Makoto tells the truth. I broke her leg with a pestle.'

'Why?'

'Because she's a witch.'

But Waziri in great excitement like a man who has with difficulty kept the truth to himself while hearing others abuse it, jumped up and waved his long arms, shouting: 'Not so, lord, it's a mistake. This man Obasa has a foolish head and his eyes are bad. He struck at the girl, true. But he did not injure her. For if so, how is it that she ran away to Shibi immediately after Ali set her free? Lord, a hundred saw her.'

In fact a score of voices from the crowd uttered loud exclamations in corroboration. They too seemed indignant that any other story should be put forward.

Bradgate remanded Obasa to prison until Aissa could be found to give evidence. His object was to keep the man out of mischief till the rains broke.

Finally he promised the Emir that the Christians would not be allowed to hold any more services in Kolu, for that year at least; and he made a little speech to the people assuring them that the rains must break soon.

'There has never been a whole year's drought in Yanrin because it is too near the sea. Moreover, I sent for food to Berua, and next week I am going to fetch it. If the merchants here put up their prices, I shall sell this at a low price. No one will be allowed to starve. Above all, you must not sell your children. I am told that some children have disappeared from

Kolu. It's a very bad thing. It is against the law to sell children on any account whatever.'

The people listened with blank faces, expressing nothing. They knew that it was not at all sure that rain would fall. History informed them that Yanrin had once been cursed by Oke so that not rain but burning cinders fell upon the land for ten years. They were convinced also that it was better to sell children at the beginning of a famine when they were strong and able to walk, than later when they were already unfit to travel; better then than to let them die. As for the unlawfulness, they knew there was no danger of punishment. For adoptions were lawful, and it was not possible to distinguish between adoption by persons desiring a child to love and cherish from one by those intending to make it a drudge or barter it to a husband or a brothel. The one couple often became the other after a few years.

It seemed to them all that Bradgate was talking nonsense, but they listened patiently and respectfully and did not think badly of him because (they said) it is his business to tell these tales. They were only perplexed to know his object. But it was generally agreed that his objection to the selling of children, as also to slavery, was religious, because there was no reasonable explanation for it.

Bradgate, having finished his little speech, which pleased him by its good sense, took leave of the Emir. The two potentates faced each other, laid their palms together, the Emir's little brown hand, dry and nervous, against the officer's nuge one; then placing them on their breasts, bowed low. The court trumpeters blew a discordant blast, the head gunman fired his six foot muzzle loader into the air with a noise like a cannon; and Bradgate with a polite gesture urged the Emir to mount before him. But the Emir would not hear of such a suggestion. He waved his hand as if to say, 'Away with such a thought,' and sinking again, stiff and old as he was, in a reverence as

117

stately as that of any old court lady, he murmured, 'Lord, king of the World, God be with you.'

'It's very kind of you, chief. I hope all are well at home. And in four days I'll be back here to begin the bridge.'

Bradgate mounted his pony with the awkward jerks of a fat man, and entirely careless of displaying to the people the large patch on the seat of his trousers or the broken brim of his hat. He began to shout at once for a felt-covered water bottle without which he never travelled. His house boy lifted it to show him. He shook his reins and moved forward. The Waziri behind beckoned fiercely to the crowd which ran forward at once to salute the judge with eager cries and gestures of affection. Even Bradgate, old soldier, cynic, practical man, was always moved by these spontaneous exhibitions of gratitude. He blushed with pleasure, and smiling, touched his hat, muttering in English in a fashion half embarrassed and half amused: 'Thanks, thanks, it's very kind of you.'

29 Ali had posted himself at the first corner about thirty yards down the road that his good-bye might be noticed. He stood, clasping the official cash book under his arm, with a dignified and calm face, until his master's eye fell upon him and he had opened his mouth to speak; but then seeing Bradgate's amused look he was carried away by his elated feelings and smiled from ear to ear. His expression was that of an English schoolboy who is conscious of having performed some great feat, a hat trick or a century, and knows that he is about to be congratulated by a friendly master.

Bradgate, who had sons of his own and liked in Ali what he liked in his own sons, saw this resemblance and it made him laugh. He pulled up and said: 'You're beginning well, boy. That was a plucky bit of work in Kolu, and as for the cash book, I can read nearly half the figures, first shot. I shall put your name in my report to the chief judge at Berua.'

Ali could not blush but he looked shy; his face grew even more shiny and his lower lip fell, showing his yellow teeth. He threw himself down on his face with a loud cry of 'Zaki.'

When Bradgate rode on he jumped up and ran after him, crying in his shrill voice, 'God bless you,' until he was breathless, but even then, kneeling and bowing by the road, he saluted until his master was out of sight. At the moment he adored Bradgate, who had appreciated him. To Ali Bradgate's praise was more valuable than that of anyone else he knew because Bradgate was the most powerful, and above all, the most feared and respected man in the neighbourhood. His words had told Ali what, like other boys newly put into the world, he most wanted to know and had the most difficulty in finding out, what he was worth. They assured him that he was a person of value, a somebody, and he was intoxicated with relief and pride. He would have died then for the man who had condescended to give him such pleasure.

When Bradgate had passed out of sight along the sandy track, he gathered up the cash book, his sign of honour, and turned back towards the camp; but being alone he forgot his dignity and broke into a trot, grinning broadly and rehearsing aloud the story he was going to tell his father: 'And he said to me, "You have done a brave deed. You are a brave man. Moreover, your numbering and writing exceeds all treasury mallams before. I shall tell the Gumna about you." '

At the corner Yerima and three of his men jumped upon him and tore away the book. Ali astonished, cried, 'But I'm Ali, Ali dan Waziri. Don't you see?'

'Yes,' the old pagan shouted, raging at him, 'We know who you are, the clever one, the white man's boy. You're the clever one who set up to teach us conduct. But you don't know everything yet. Put him down and take his guts out.'

119

Luckily Waziri had expected something like this. He arrived now with his own servants, and bellowing to Yerima, 'That's the way, quite right, only let me,' he set upon Ali with his own hands, tore his gown from him, threw him down, and beat him with his riding whip.

Ali, surprised and terrified, at first tried to catch his father's gown or feet, crying out, 'What is it, what is it? Why?'

But Waziri, furious with his panic and disappointment, beat him with all his might, shouting: 'That will teach you, you young fool. You want to ruin yourself, do you. What, you're a great man already. Ask Yerima's pardon. Ask him for your life.'

Yerima was not satisfied until the boy had been beaten unconscious. He was ill for some time. Bradgate was told that he had gone into French country to visit a sick uncle. But what surprised everybody and angered Waziri was that the public humiliation did Ali no good at all. He bore himself with even more dignity than before; and especially in the presence of those who had seen him thrashed and heard him cry out, carried his nose in the air. But when the unhappy Waziri complained of his stubbornness and folly Mallam Illo said: 'Didn't I tell you he would be spoilt at the white man's school?'

30 The Waziri was praised for his management of the trials at Akoko, but it was Owule's son Ije who earned most credit. This boy, not more than eighteen, having come to give witness against the Christians, recognized Ishe in the crowd. She was pushing towards Bradgate and shouting that Moshalo had stolen her child.

This boldness in the woman took everybody by surprise; people made way for her, and she would certainly have reached Bradgate had not Ije, calling upon two of Yerima's servants, seized her, gagged her with a piece of cloth, tied her up there and then and run her into the bush.

This was done in the sight of three or four hundred persons, including constables, mallam-secretaries, rich merchants, Christians and Christian sympathizers, garrison police, and Bradgate's servants, of whom Jamesu was chatting with Jacob within a few yards. If Bradgate had turned his head he would have seen the three men struggling with Ishe, but he had no reason for looking round just then and none of the spectators uttered the faintest cry of protest or warning. When Ije, glaring fiercely round him in his fear of some traitor, passed his eyes over them, the men turned away their heads or looked downwards and licked their lips, afraid lest some fault should be found with them even for watching the crime. Jacob, playing the part of superior person, laughed and called in Yoruba the proverb, 'I take you woman, I do not like you, woman.'

Jamesu, delighted with his friend's boldness, complimented him with his usual guffaw and the cry, 'Oh, you bad boy, Jacob,' but no one else dared so much as to smile. They felt as guilty and frightened as dogs when one of the pack is being thrashed.

The three men dragged Ishe into the bush, put her on a horse and took her to Kolu, where they thrust her into a house. In a few minutes she heard Numi's voice. Ije came in, untied her arms, took out the gag; she was let out and ran to her son, who received her calmly and without any sign of welcome. He was eating a honey cake and carried in his hand a new toy bow. He showed his mother the bow and said that the kind woman had given it to him.

Ije and Owule's youngest wife Shabeya now came in and began to tell how Numi had been found, and to admire him. What a nice boy he was. They explained why it had been necessary to prevent her from making a complaint to the judge, because the judge was a Christian, and wanted an excuse to

121

put Owule in prison. He would have affected to believe that Numi had been kidnapped for sacrifice. Then he would destroy the juju house and the country would be ruined by the angry gods.

Ishe, having been fed, understood this very well. Like other country people she flattered herself on knowing the corruption and wickedness of all men and especially those in authority.

Ije and Shabeya complimented her, fed her, and caressed Numi for the whole day, letting her perceive that they did this in order to be reconciled with her and to prevent her from making complaints against them. Ishe, half drunk with good food and drink, with flattery and with the joy of having Numi safe before her eyes, winked at them and said every few minutes, 'You're being very nice to me, aren't you?' and laughed in their faces.

Thus she preserved her country self-respect. She showed these townspeople that they could not make a fool of her.

In the evening drums were brought, a feast was given, and after the feast, a dance in propitiation of Oke. All were drunk, including Ishe and Numi. Numi was asleep, but Ishe danced among the other women, beating themselves and screeching: 'Forgive us, Oke. Have pity, we are yours.' Old withered grandmothers afraid that their children would starve and young girls already hungry, tore themselves with their nails and shrieked repentance for any fault which they might have committed. They beat their heads on the floor, on the rough mud of the walls which cut their faces; Ishe, her forehead streaming with blood into her eyes, stamped and wriggled for two hours without ceasing, echoing the same cry: 'Have pity, Oke. I give you all, have pity.'

Ije and Shabeya, conscious of their sins, began to weep and howl like jackals, sometimes in despair, sometimes in rage. All were filled, as they wept, with the consciousness of guilt.

A cry was heard, 'Who gives a child to Oke?' and repeated a hundred times to the rhythm of the drums. Ishe, prompted with the test began to scream: 'Oke, pity your people, send the rain. Don't kill them, Oke. I give you all, Oke. I give you myself, my body, my breasts, my womb.'

Owule came up to her and said: 'I thank you, Ishe—you save us—you love Oke—you love this poor people dying of hunger—you give a sacrifice to Oke.'

The woman, who could not understand anything, screeched more loudly: 'Sacrifice for Oke, sacrifice for Oke.'

Owule said to her: 'What will please Oke—what will satisfy her after all our wickedness and bad treatment of her. Something very good, something that costs much. Because we have been very bad people.'

'Yes, we have been bad people.'

'Only a pure virgin freely given with the heart—only that will satisfy Oke.'

'Given with the heart.'

'You are a good woman, Ishe. Everyone respects you. You love this poor people. You are brave and generous. You save them from Oke's anger.'

'I save them, yes, I save them.'

'You give Numi.'

Ishe did not answer. Owule brought beer and she drank it thirstily like water. The sweat was pouring from her. Her legs failed and she tumbled down. The drummers came round her and beat over her body, which writhed and jerked to the music. She jumped up and ran about screaming: 'Pity us—Oke, forgive—send rain before we die'; then ran against the wall and cut her head open but did not faint.

They gave her more beer, and Owule said: 'Brave Ishe, you save us, you help us, you give all—you give Numi.'

The woman sighed: 'I give all—I give Numi.'

Owule and Ije caught her by the arms and ran her to the grove where the big Oke mound of Kolu has stood for many hundreds of years.

They pressed her to her knees before the mound and passed a rope over the back of her neck and under her knees, securing her in the posture of adoration and sacrifice. Her arms were pulled out in front of her and her hands tied. She was still crying out: 'I give all to Oke,' but as they had expected, the influence of the music, the songs and prayers and beer and the encouragement of the Oke dancers was already failing and she made efforts to straighten her back and to rise from the floor.

'What are you doing?' she asked them. 'Let me go.'

An assistant came running with Numi on his shoulders. The boy, newly wakened from sleep, rubbed his eyes and, seeing his mother, uttered a grunt of satisfaction.

Owule and Ije thrust him quickly feet forward into the loop of Ishe's arms so that he sat on her folded knees. She clasped him tightly to keep him safe and to console herself in her fear and her guilty confusion.

The boy now fully awake, and frightened to see his mother tied, and by the solemn looks of Owule and his two assistants, began to struggle and cry. Ishe also struggled and uttered a piercing scream. The assistant Gani put his hands to the side of her neck and compressed the veins until she was faint and almost unconscious. Ije then took Numi by the ears, and standing sidelong pulled his head forward and downwards towards the Oke mound. Owule struck off the boy's head with a matchet and the blood spurted upon the Oke mound. Afterwards Ishe was thrown into the river. Owule had not wished to kill Ishe. It was necessary to do so only because she had tried to complain to the white man and might do so again, and thus bring further trouble to the Church of Ifa and Oke. But all who took part in the murder of the poor woman felt guilty and ashamed, and hated the white man for it.

31 The offering of Numi was known within twelve hours to everyone in Yanrin except Bradgate, and gave much satisfaction. Ishe was praised for her self-sacrifice, and many people young and old, especially women, feeling the desire to do as well or better, offered themselves, their children, and their favourite possessions to Oke. One young girl of fourteen in Kolu, intelligent and warm-hearted beyond her years, cut herself so badly in devotion to the goddess that she died.

On the second day after the sacrifice a thunderstorm broke in the Shibi hills and scattered one quick shower over Yanrin. This was claimed joyfully by Owule and his priests for Oke's work. But Carr in chapel the next morning returned thanks to God for his answer to the people's prayers, and many farmers in Berua and Shibi sent presents to the mission. In Yanrin also, where Aissa was thought to be the greatest and known to be the most powerful among the Christians, the credit was given to her. Within twenty-four hours of the thunderstorm three children, playing on Yanrin market place under the prison wall, were heard singing:

'Owule fell and the rain fell,
The blood ran out of Owule
And the rain out of the sky.'

The children were taken up, but they declared the song to be an old one. They had heard it yesterday. Yerima sent orders that all who repeated it should be arrested and beaten, but by this time half the people were singing that when Owule fell, the rain fell.

Everyone who heard the argument knew that it was true and saw the logic of it. They saw Owule falling down in Kolu market, and then at once the dark rain fall from the sky. Ten

125

days had elapsed between Aissa's knocking down of Owule and the shower of rain. They knew this, but they forgot it in the desire to make truth irresistible. For they said, 'This is obviously true and therefore it should be believed by everybody.' Practical men were the more anxious to confirm the truth because, as commonly happens, the drought so long established had not been broken by one storm. The farmers, struck by panic, were shouting that it was time some god or other helped them. In one village a mob chased Owule's sons out of the place, threatening to murder them if more rain did not fall within a week. Another man was caught beating an Oke mound with a whip and cursing her for a swindler. He was arrested and flogged, but it was said that other mounds had been insulted and no one taken.

Some women beating a floor were heard singing:

> 'The white god is angry with Oke.
> He gets no yam, no sheep.
> The white god is stronger than Oke.
> He has stopped up her rain.'

And this too was known to be a fact. For the white priest at Shibi was still praying to God to send more rain and plenty at a time.

Everyone in Yanrin began to sing:

> 'The white god is angry with Oke
> And Owule the priest.
> The white god calls for blood
> For blood He gives rain.'

Yerima and the pagans knew their danger and fought to save themselves. They offered a large reward for the discovery of the Christian fugitives in Yanrin and double for Aissa.

Every house in Kolu was searched and every person and animal accounted for. Indeed, in the hurry of the day, two pie

126

bitches which, as it turned out, had owners to swear to them, were killed in mistake for Christians. But everyone, even the bravest, was apt to be startled by the movements of any yellow dog near him, for it was believed that both Aissa and Umaru were lurking somewhere in the place.

32 In fact Aissa and Umaru had escaped some days before. Aissa, having made her way north to Daji country, was ferried over by an islander who knew and cared nothing about Yanrin politics. She begged her way to Shibi in a week. Umaru was hidden by some Christian sympathizers in Kolu, who smuggled him over on the first black night. They did not, however, go directly to the mission, but to Ojo's compound on the Shibi road.

Ojo's compound was a large ruinous house on the outskirts of the town, between town and mission. Most missions, like all barracks, whether of police or soldiers, have private meeting places outside the official boundary; sometimes in the nearest town, sometimes in the bush; club houses where the members can amuse themselves, discuss, argue, dress and play exactly as they choose, away from the foreigners' eye. Soldiers can take off their uniforms, clerks their shoes and coats, women can scream and wave their arms, everyone can laugh, shout, dance in the native style without losing the respect and confidence of white colleagues and friends.

It is in the mission club house, which may be a fallen log in the jungle, or a dry river bed, that Christian ideas are most eagerly discussed and the Bible searched for information and prophecies. At Ojo's compound, which he had taken over as a derelict from a pagan family destroyed by the influenza in 1918, not only the mission people but many from the town came to talk about religion, to hold prayer meetings of their own, to ask advice from Ojo and the other mission leaders, and especially to consult the oracle.

There were two oracles in Shibi, the big answer and the little. The little which cost anything from a few cowrie shells to sixpence was a text chosen at random from the Bible by anybody who could read, that is to say Ojo, old Sara, who was the senior woman, Frederick or Mrs. Carr's small boy, Jimmy. A big answer was a scroll from the Christian Honeycomb of Truth, and it cost a dollar, that is, a florin.

A Honeycomb is a small flat box divided into compartments not much bigger than honey cells. Each cell contains a text from the old or new Testament printed on thin paper and rolled up so tightly that once extracted from its place it cannot be put back again.

When Aissa reached the compound at about half-past five it was crowded with the whole native population of the mission and their friends from Shibi. The former were massed in a dense ring about Ojo, Nagulo and some others who were carrying on a lively dispute, the latter were chattering and pushing to and fro, no one would pay any attention to Aissa, who was asking for Gajere, of whom most of them had never heard. Neither did these townspeople recognize her. She had not been a renowned person at her departure, and moreover, she had then been plump and good-looking, always neatly dressed in a blouse and cloth. Now she was stark naked and very thin. Her head had been shaved in prison, and this had altered its proportion to her face. The skull appeared no larger than a coconut, but her large swollen lips protruding from her hollow cheeks were enormous, her eyes were bloodshot and her skin blackened by dirt and bruises. As she knelt on all fours in the gateway her long flat breasts almost touched the ground; her knees were tied up in bloody rags and her short leg, bandaged at the stump with a large bundle of tobacco leaves, dragged behind her. She was taken for some beggar or leper by those whom she tried to stop; they brushed past her in a hurry to hear the oracle.

Ever since the riot and trials at Akoko the mission had been full of indignation with Bradgate and the pagans. The Carrs had some reason to be angry, for they were convinced that Aissa and Umaru had been murdered, and Hilda Carr especially could not hide her feelings from her pupils, who were therefore encouraged to be angry by the knowledge that it was the right thing. Ojo, as might have been expected, was the most bitter. He spoke in such a manner of Bradgate, calling him a servant of the devil and a murderer, that Carr was obliged to reprove him, but he answered that Bradgate was condemned by God himself because he was a judge. Had not God written: Judge not.

No one could help being fond of Ojo because of his keenness and his passionate desire to do something great and important. When the news came that Bradgate had forbidden any more meetings in Kolu he saw at once an opportunity to distinguish himself and asked for leave to hold a meeting in Yanrin itself.

Carr told him that Yanrin was also out of bounds.

'But, sah, if de spirit tell me to go, I hear de spirit, I no hear dat Bradgate.'

'Why, Ojo, you know you can't go. You'd only get yourself murdered like the others.'

But the boy was too excited to be frightened. 'Sah,' he cried, 'you doan see. If de rain come now in Yanrin, dem priests say dey make it. De people no fit know we make it. Dey no give tanks to God, sah. Dey no come here to church.'

Carr smiled and remarked, 'You think they're going to cheat us.'

'Sah, sah, I go to Yanrin, pray der, den all dem bad pagans fit to follow Jesus.'

129

Carr was amused by this simple view of things, but he answered the boy: 'It's not for us to know why God sends the rain or keeps it back, Ojo. I shouldn't make any promises about it.'

'No, sah, I no make promises. I tell em when tree men come together, pray to God, he gib em all ting dey want.'

'In His own time, Ojo.'

Ojo, checked, stood staring with round eyes and open wet lips; then with a glance of suspicion asked, 'Does it say dat for Bible, sah?'

'That is meant, of course.'

Ojo confused and as it were extinguished by this authority went away in silence. But in ten minutes his shrill voice could be heard again from the boys' compound, exhorting, arguing, beseeching in his own language.

He was explaining that Carr was afraid to go to Yanrin because of the judge, but that he would go.

'When the judge is in Berua, I'll go,' he shouted. 'I'll go and tell these fools their god is a silly fool's god, a black man's god. Who will go fight for Jesus' sake?'

No one volunteered. Even Shangoedi was afraid of the Kolua. But as soon as Umaru came back he gave his support; Nagulo as usual followed his example; and then many others, moved by the spirit, offered themselves. They demanded only a favourable oracle.

33 The little oracle had been consulted every day and many times a day, but the answers, as usual contradictory and perplexing, had proved very difficult to interpret.

One evening Sara had this reply to a question asked of Mister Carr's own Bible borrowed by Frederick during dinner time from the bedroom.

'Thinkest thou that I cannot pray to my father and he shall presently give me more than twelve legions of angels.'

Umaru declared that this was a favourable answer because it meant that the angels would fight for them in Kolu, and he was supported by Nagulo, but the prudent Brimah objected that it was not clear enough, and that as angels were women they could not fight. He demanded still another oracle, a big one, and Ojo, feeling with his demagogue's instinct, the instinct of a herd animal, where the weight of popular inclination lay, supported him. For he was confident that his god would give him a favourable answer. Umaru, who never cared to raise his voice in dispute, said little, but the other three, each with his friends and disciples, equally enraged, were shouting at the tops of their voices. Nagulo had the loudest voice, but Ojo, his eyes rolling till the whites could be seen all round the iris, his mouth opening so wide that all his teeth glittered between his black lips, his thin arms swinging like branches in a gale, was the most forcible. His gestures were more eloquent than Nagulo's shouts, his upturned eyes exclaimed, 'What nonsense,' his flopping hands swept arguments away and made their place clean, his pouting lips and pushed forward head seemed to exclaim, 'The man's a perfect fool.'

He too began to shout. All shouted together, raging as if they would tear each other. But Ojo's screaming voice outlasted all the rest, and suddenly Nagulo gave way.

'Ask dem box den,' he sighed. 'Go get dem box—dem stool. Dey no good, but ask dem.'

Shangoedi and Sara, the two eldest of the women, were sent for the box and Ojo's stool. This stool of soft carved wood was always used for a big asking and it was itself sacred. It was often used to confer fertility on women. Even pagan women were glad to pay sixpence to rub their stomachs upon it. It was also considered good for leprosy, various skin diseases and suppurating wounds. When this stool, blackened with grease

131

and blood stains, had been brought to the compound, all the people fell on their knees and Ojo, kneeling also, placed upon it the box, opened to show the honeycomb. Then holding over it a crochet hook pointing downwards he closed his eyes and prayed: 'Almighty God, our Fader, you our fader, love your poor people, we all fit to die for you, you our fader and mudder, Almighty God, you know all ting, you know dat de bad pagans Ajala and Owule do all tings against de Christians, O God, nutting is hid from you sight. O Fader, you tell us now if it be you will we go to Yanrin fight dis bad pagan Owule, for Jesus Christ's sake, you good son, Amen.'

He then plunged the hook downwards into the honeycomb and drew up on the point a roll of paper which uncoiled itself in the air. Amid a deep silence, he reverently detached the paper from the hook, stretched it flat on the chair seat and read: 'The Son of man shall send forth his angels and they shall gather out of his kingdom all things that offend and them which do iniquity and shall cast them into a furnace of fire.'

He read in English. Voices shouted at once: 'What is it, what did God say, what are we to do.'

Ojo himself was perplexed by the oracle and read it over several times. The others forgetting all their feelings of reverence crowded round him, jostling the stool, pushing the women aside, reaching for the paper itself.

Ojo translated the message into Yoruba, Umaru into Fulani. A furious discussion broke out. He says, 'Seize his enemies, burn them up, the cursed pagans,' Nagulo shouted, and his friend Salé agreed with him: 'That's it, we must set fire to Kolu, friends, you heard, that's what God says, burn them up, the bastards.'

'All his angels will help us.'

'That's it, friends. See how they helped us this last time. Not one of us hurt. What a miracle.'

Brimah, the carrier, a man known for his good sense, smiled

132

and said: 'What about the police?' meaning the government police, armed with carbines, 'Suppose they shoot.'

But Nagulo laughed at him. 'They can't hurt us after we drink Jesus' blood.'

'Can't they? Have you tried?'

Shangoedi flew at him: 'You fool, did Jesus die, could they kill him? Jesus' blood cannot die.'

'I'm told that he did die.'

'What, he lay down in a hole, he laughed at them. Then in three days he jumped up.' And she jumped into the air, waved her arms and grimaced.

Brimah smiled and shrugged his shoulders as if to say: 'What fools they are,' then shouted angrily, 'All right, go and get killed.'

Suddenly Umaru spoke and at once all were silent. The Fulani had the prestige of a brave man. He said coolly: 'When Bradgate goes away to Berua, I shall burn the juju house at Ketemfe. I shall go even alone.'

'Why,' cried Brimah, 'don't you know there are a thousand demons in that wood. You'll be killed, that's all.'

'What matter. I shall kill some of God's enemies first, and those who die doing God's works enter Paradise. It seems to me that Paradise is worth getting in exchange for a country like this.'

The leper Kalé attending with an eager excited face cried joyfully: 'Yes, that's a good place. It will be good among the angels of God.'

But the tall Fulani who had seen the cripple running away in Kólu market place looked down on him with contempt and said: 'The angels are reserved for fighting men. Everybody knows that.' He marched away.

34 The dispute went on for a long time because everyone was arguing about different questions. Ojo wanted to go direct to Kolu as before and hold a meeting where he could preach his famous sermon; but Nagulo was urging, 'Let us go to-night,' and Shangoedi was screaming, 'We must kill Musa and Ali. They are the accursed ones, the enemies of Jesus.'

'Yes, and all the rich,' another cried.

'All judges, God has cursed them.'

'What, and the white man?'

'Yes, those are the worst. Does Belly ever go to church? The judges are all enemies of Jesus.'

Ojo shouting for silence and unable to make himself obeyed, fell on his knees and began to pray to God for help in bringing the Kolua to know the truth.

But suddenly the hubbub was cut short by a shriek so long and loud that all turned towards it. Aissa was seen lying on the ground with her face against the juju stool.

Sara, the old matron, sitting beside the girl and gently stroking her bald head, looked up through her crooked spectacles and said calmly, 'I tell Aissa what God says.'

'Aissa, is it Aissa?'

'Yes, Aissa came and ask me where Abba and Gajere, and I tell her they no come here, and then I tell her what God says.'

'But the answer wasn't for her, Sara.'

'Yes, it was for her, friens. Dat's why you doan understand it. It's because you doan know who God talking to. But God talk to Aissa.'

Sara's opinion was always treated with respect because she could read. She had besides the authority of goodness. All

134

listened while she spoke in her mild, reproachful voice. 'He spoke plain if you hear him. God always speak plain. Aissa come here, she wan know where Gajere and Abba. She find em (look for them) everywhere—no one fit to tell her. Den God speak, he say to Aissa he take all workers of iniquity. We all know Gajere bad man. God say he take all tings dat offend. You know Abba bastard chile, got bad spirit. God say he put dem bad men bad tings for de fire. He put Gajere and Abba in hell. Dat's what God says. God always speaks plain, it's you ears doan hear proper.'

This explanation was true on the face of it, so obvious that all were convinced in a moment. Cries of wonder and praise broke out on all sides. Many, overwhelmed by their sense of God's nearness, fell on their knees.

35 Meanwhile Ojo had run to welcome Aissa. He embraced her with tears of pity and joy. He had forgiven her cruel desertion, her backsliding. 'Aissa, ma dear, you come back to Jesus now. We go to Kolu togedder, we testify to Jesus.'

But Aissa, hearing the name of Kolu, began to struggle and cried out: No, no, she wouldn't go to Kolu. She wouldn't go near those bad pagans. She wouldn't do anything. She wanted to be left alone.

Ojo, who was kneeling face to face with her in the midst of the singers who now pressed about the pair, tried to hold the hysterical girl in his arms, imploring her to listen to him. 'Aissa, Aissa, I sorry for you. You done lose dem babe. But why God take him away. Because he see you love dem babe too much, you go way from him, you go way from Jesus. Now he give you dis bad trouble, he bring you to him.'

'No, no, no,' Aissa shrieked. 'I no belong to Jesus now. I no want him, I no love him no more.'

'Aissa, dats the debbil speak from your heart. You catch the debbil inside you. You drive out dem bad debbil, Aissa.'

But Aissa, struggling, biting, scratching, screamed: 'Yes, I catch debbil—I want debbil. I curse you, Jesus, you Ojo.'

Cries of horror broke out from the crowd and when Aissa, tearing herself from Ojo, fell sideways near the front row of women they scattered away from her.

But just then the sentry on the road called out: 'The master coming.'

Instantly all was quiet. The mission people slipped into the huts, the townspeople out of the side towards Shibi; Umaru and Ojo catching up Aissa carried her into the bush behind the compound; she fought them fiercely, twisting in their hands like a bundle of snakes; tearing at them with her nails, shrieking as if she were on fire.

'I curse you, I curse dem Carrs, I curse Jesus.'

They threw her into a deserted hut and Umaru stifled her screams with a cloth. But Ojo, more tender-hearted, loving the girl whom he had saved before, was in great distress. He tried to catch her hands, implored her: 'Drive out dem spirit, Aissa. Doan fight against Jesus. For he want you now. He waiting for you, Aissa. You let him in your heart, he make you happy.'

Aissa knew that she had a bad spirit in her but she did not care. She did not want to drive it out. She liked it because it gave her pain and told her to be angry. She had done many wicked things. She had offended Jesus and God and the Holy Spirit, and probably many other spirits too. She had brought down the wrath of all three upon Gajere and Abba. She was abominably wicked, and if people were not careful she would even die.

As soon as the Carrs were past Ojo and Sara prayed for Aissa. The whole mission reproached her for her obstinate devil. Then it was offended and said to her: 'Now you may die,

136

Aissa,' and at once she set herself to die. By the next morning everyone could see that she was dying. Her eyes were dull, her skin was grey. She lay curled up among her rags in the corner, her face to the wall. No one could get anything from her except the words spoken in deep sulky anger: 'I bad, I go die.'

For several hours everyone in the mission was in great excitement. What would happen now? Would the Carrs discover Aissa? Would they find out that Ojo had been consulting the oracle? What would Ojo do then? But during the course of the day not only Aissa but the Kolu project was forgotten in the arrival of a new harmonium by eight carriers from Berua. Mrs. Carr was heard to say that even the big church at Berua had not so good or expensive an harmonium, and Shangoedi who hated the Berua people, traditional enemies of Yanrin, gave praise at every service with such warmth of joy and devotion that she brought on one of her fits.

36 Aissa would certainly have died if it had not been for some Yanrin spy in Shibi, who betrayed her and Umaru to the council there.

Yerima and the council were delighted at the opportunity not only of catching the dangerous Umaru and the witch, but of setting Bradgate against the Carrs. Waziri was sent off hot foot with a couple of his most trustworthy agents to intercept Bradgate, who had crossed that afternoon at Shibi; and by hard galloping he reached the ferry before dark. But as all the boats had been used to carry the officer and his labourers and some had not returned yet, it was eight before he reached the rest house, about a mile up river from the mission, and there he was told that the judge was dining with the Carrs. The house boy Mama, who was Waziri's chief spy in the mission, anxious to soften this bad news, explained that Bradgate had not wished to visit the Carrs, but that they had come for him. 'Yes, the woman too, though she is seven months big and lame, she walked the whole road until she had lost all her breath and was ready to die. She begged him with tears and so at last he consented.' Mama exaggerated in order to please the anxious Waziri, who knew very well that any failure on his part was likely to ruin him and Ali too; but it was true that Bradgate had intended to avoid the Carrs.

His excuse was to be that he had arrived late and must go early, and he took care to make his landing on the other side of the town, out of sight from the mission. But he had scarcely set foot on the beach before the Carrs appeared, the little man in a clean white suit, his wife in an elaborate muslin frock which looked absurd on a woman in her condition. Both were extremely hot and Mrs. Carr, who seemed very ill, whose white cheeks, streaming with sweat, had fallen in like an old woman's, was in such distress for breath that Bradgate thought she would faint and began to call angrily to the boys, still afloat, to bring a chair.

But the woman, trying to smile, waved her hand to show that she did not want a chair, and gasped reproachfully, 'Mister Bradgate, what a shame—to slip past like this—we opened the Christmas stores as soon as we heard you were coming.'

She put on great indignation, and Carr, too, though as usual less demonstrative than his wife, remarked that he hoped Bradgate had not intended to avoid them altogether.

'At least you must come to dinner,' cried Hilda, 'because it's all ordered for you.'

'It's awfully good of you, Mrs. Carr, but all this is giving you a lot of trouble.' Already he was melting to their kindness.

'You know very well we're simply delighted—why, it's months since we've seen you.'

Bradgate knew of course that this unusual warmth of greeting was due simply to the fact that he had been quarrelling with the Carrs. They were being Christian to him. But he knew also that there was no more hypocrisy in their eagerness than in any display of hospitality; probably less, for they were really troubled by the thought that he looked upon them as enemies; that he was trying to avoid them.

He accepted the invitation as one impossible to refuse, and he was amused with himself to see the elaborate meal devised by Mrs. Carr and probably, as she had said, taken from the special stores reserved for birthdays and feast days; the hors d'œuvres, bottled soup, tinned entrées, ashantee fowl, plum pudding were intended to soften his heart, but he was touched nevertheless. A grown person is moved by a child's naïf attempts to make friends after some falling out by the offer of a sweet and some insinuating smiles and wriggles. It is only the stupidest and blindest who says to such a child: 'Yes, I know what all these smiles are for, but they don't take me in.' Bradgate certainly was incapable of such folly and meanness.

The Carrs' strategy was amusing, but it expressed real feeling which charmed a lonely man, so that many times during the meal, while he was telling stories, making jokes, chatting with Carr about the news from home and Mrs. Carr about market prices and his scheme for importing grain into Yanrin, he thought: 'They really are good, these people; there is a lot in Christianity, whatever you say.'

He looked at little Mrs. Carr while she coquetted absurdly with him; smiling in a roguish manner which did not suit her at all and calling in a shrill voice apropos of his last mild joke about the Nigerian egg: 'Oh, but how naughty of you, Captain Bradgate.'

She was probably about twenty-five and she had been a pretty girl, intelligent, high spirited, fond of dances and games. Now she had the complexion and wrinkles of an old woman. She had been married four years and she had buried her first baby, somewhere down river, within a year of her marriage. Now she was to have another, at home, so he gathered, but she refused to leave her work for another month and already she was exhausted, scarcely able to walk. She had thrown away her looks and health, comfort and security, all amusements, all the things considered worth having by other women; she had sacrificed one child's life and she was risking another's and her own, in order, as she would put it, to bring the truth to these people, for the love of Jesus.

Or perhaps for the love of her husband, Bradgate thought; and as for him, it's his job. But they do it well and it's a noble job. And he exclaimed: 'By jove, plum pudding. Not plum pudding?'

'Do you like Christmas pudding? When you come back from Berua, we'll open the other case,' cried she.

'And brandy; not brandy?' Bradgate, who knew that the Carrs were teetotallers, was astonished to see the bottle, it was true, a medicine bottle, offered him by the small boy.

'Ah! that's especially for you—but you mustn't tell anybody,' cried Mrs. Carr with a gallant look which nearly made Bradgate laugh; at the same time it moved him to such sentimental feelings of tenderness and admiration for the little woman with her pinched cheeks and little red nose that his own air and expression while he bowed and smiled at her was not less ridiculous. He was conscious of it; he caught Carr's eye fixed upon him with a genial but amused look; but he did not care what he seemed like. He was too much moved. He cried out with most sincere feeling: 'Now I call that real hospitality.'

It was at this moment that Waziri's voice was heard bellowing from the pitch darkness beyond the verandah rails, 'Zaki, Zaki.'

'Someone for you,' Carr said.

'What, what! Who's there?'

'Lord, Waziri.'

'What do you want?'

'I have news, important news.'

'But, Waziri, you see I am at dinner and this is not my house.'

'Pardon, Lord, but this is very important news.'

Bradgate apologized to the Carrs and asked leave to hear Waziri. 'Come up, then, you old rascal, and tell me your latest yarn.'

Bradgate did not usually call Waziri an old rascal. He used this tone only because it was the right one for a cheerful dinner party.

Waziri appearing in the light cast by the pink candles on the verandah floor saluted deeply and muttered: 'It's secret, lord, I can't speak here.'

Bradgate apologizing again to the Carrs moved his chair to the side of the verandah. But he was annoyed by the interruption, and his displeasure was not removed by the discovery that Waziri had come only to try and persuade him to go back to Yanrin; and to make the usual charges against the Christians; that they were corrupting the people, stirring up revolution; that they had threatened the pagan priests and wanted to burn the juju house.

He answered brusquely that all these matters had been settled. The Christians could not be turned out of Shibi because Shibi was not in Yanrin. Besides, they had a right to preach their religion there.

'But, Lord, if they make trouble?'

'Then we'll run them in, but till then we can't do anything. You know that quite well. How can we arrest people simply for their religion, whatever it is.'

141

'Then if they break the law we can tie them up?'

'Of course, of course.'

'And if this white mallam break the law?'

'What do you mean?'

'Lord, they have hidden very bad criminals that you have been seeking. Umaru and Aissa are both hidden here.'

'I don't believe it. Somebody has been telling you lies.'

'Lord, I can prove it.'

'Then show your proof, but it had better be a good one. Understand this, that Mr. and Mrs. Carr are my friends and I won't have them annoyed for nothing. Go now and salute your master. Tell him I don't want any more complaints against the Christians. If the Christians and the pagans fight it's his business to stop them. That's what he's for. Good night, Waziri.'

Waziri continued to implore, even to shout. He was in despair. He saw himself ruined. But Bradgate sent him away.

For a long time his voice could be heard as he retreated slowly towards the town, lamenting to the stars and to Allah, the difficulties of a waziri and the follies of judges.

37 The same evening about ten o'clock when Bradgate, escorted by the Carrs and the two lantern boys, his own and theirs, was strolling back to his own quarters at the rest house, and all three were laughing very much at a story told by Mrs. Carr out of a *Punch* sent by Bradgate himself to the mission three weeks before, he was accosted on the outside of the village by Waziri, who with excited gestures and cries made him step to the side of the road and look over the mud wall of a compound. It was full of mission men and women who appeared, as far as could be told by the light of the fire and two or three lanterns, to be quarrelling furiously.

He heard Mrs. Carr murmuring in her anxious voice: 'Oh yes, some of our people do come here in the evening, and they always make such a noise.'

They were in fact making such a noise and shouting at each other with such frantic rage that not one of them noticed the three white faces peering over the mats.

Waziri and one of his agents, an emaciated old man in rags, who looked even more desperate and ravaged than his master, each carrying a torch of straw, rushed into the compound by the back doorway and caught two of the most violent contestants, a skeleton of a woman, foaming and panting with excitement, and a burly looking Yoruba; one to each hand. Both turning angrily and seeing Bradgate were at once silenced. They stared with bulging, terrified eyes. The whole compound fell into silence so that Mrs. Carr could be heard saying: 'I like to see them enjoying themselves.'

'Look!' Waziri bellowed. 'Look, lord, this one is Nagulo who struck Gani and this is Shangoedi who says she will destroy the rulers of Yanrin and there (pointing with his chin at the tall Fulani, who in the palsied grip of the ancient secret service man, stood impassive and apparently bored) Umaru, who stabbed Moshalo, and this very night he has sworn to burn the juju house at Ketemfe.'

At this the trembling old agent exclaimed in a hoarse deep voice: 'It's true, by Allah, I heard him myself; and the witch that struck down Owule and made the rain, she's here too.'

'Aissa too!' Waziri roared. 'All the malefactors whom you sought are here, lord. The white priest has hidden them. This is a great wrong.'

Bradgate was surprised, for although it is well known in Nigeria that criminals seek refuge in the missions to gain a white man's support, and magistrates cannot expect the missionaries to betray their converts, he had not thought that Carr, after writing angry letters about the misdeeds of the Kolua, would hide such blackguards as Nagulo and Umaru. But he had no intention of repaying his hospitality by making trouble for him with the resident of the province and possibly the bishop; besides, he did not wish to take anything at a mission very seriously. After gazing for a minute with some astonishment he remarked: 'So this is where all my runaway murderers go to.'

His joking tone and his use of the word murderer, whereas no one had committed anything as bad as murder, made everyone see that he was joking. The whole compound burst into a shout of laughter, and Nagulo, rolling on his knees with laughter like a child, cried out in English, 'Oh, sah, you kill me for fun.'

'Yes,' said Bradgate severely, 'but I ought to send you to prison.'

This caused a sudden doubt. Once more there was silence, anxious glances. But Bradgate having prefaced the way for another joke to crown his going half turned to Mrs. Carr and concluded: 'Only if I hang the worst of you, you blackguards, Mrs. Carr will lose all her favourites.'

Mrs. Carr, who was not quick to understand a joke and had stood pale and a little confused, said earnestly, 'They are so splendid, Mr. Bradgate, you don't realize——'

But her voice was overwhelmed by another shout of laughter from the compound, which after an instant's hesitation had seen by Bradgate's own smile that he was again making a joke.

Bradgate delighted with this success chose the moment to make his farewell. He brushed aside the Carrs' explanations and apologies: 'Don't mention it; of course you didn't know; you've been extremely good to me, Mrs. Carr (grasping the lady's hand and bending towards her), I can't thank you enough. I shall look forward to seeing you on my way back. So don't forget the pudding and the brandy sauce.'

He marched away in front of his lantern boy with the air of a man turning with credit from amusement to business.

Carr, however, was not the less angry with his people, and especially Nagulo, Ojo, and Brimah. He suspected them of holding one of these juju meetings which are the bane of African missionaries, and he wanted to know where Umaru had been hidden for the last three weeks, and if it was true that Aissa was there too. But Ojo, who had bolted at the first alarm, could not be found; and the others gave evasive answers.

No one knew anything about Aissa. No one had seen or heard of her.

'She die for Yanrin, sah. Dey kill her for Yanrin.'

They were afraid to tell him where she was in case he should be angry with them for letting the girl lie untended.

Carr searched the compound, which was surrounded by half-ruined huts used formerly for carriers' barracks, but he did not find Aissa, who had been carried into the town.

But about two in the morning Frederick's dog began to bark and Frederick was heard shouting at somebody; the women began to scream that the hyenas were in the camp. Jim the small boy joined in the dispute on one side and Brimah on the other.

'I no fit wake em for dis time,' the cook shouted.

But Mrs. Carr, who had lately become a very light sleeper, was seen on her verandah, standing in the moonlight, her broad striped pyjamas thrust into yellow mosquito boots and her thin pig tail twisted under the collar of her dressing gown; and Ojo, pushing Frederick aside, rushed at her shouting excitedly that Aissa was very sick, she was dying; they didn't know what to do with her.

'Kolua go kill Gajere and Abba. She catch bad spirit. She go die now. She no care for nutting.'

'Why didn't you tell me before, Ojo?'

145

'We tink if Bradgate go hear he take her for prison. You come now, ma; she very sick.'

Hilda's irritation and weariness had already vanished in anxiety for her favourite. She told the boys to be quiet, not to wake her husband, and sent Frederick at once for the medicine box and a lantern.

She found Aissa in a small isolated hut, dirty and stinking, among the rubbish heaps at the edge of the town. The girl was lying on the bare floor and at first glance seemed to be dead. Her fixed eyes did not move when the light flashed on them; her cheeks and stomach had fallen in; her mouth hung open.

She showed no sign of hearing the questions Hilda asked her; but she was breathing and her pulse could be felt. She had no fever. There appeared nothing wrong with her except a few bruises, dirt, emaciation. The stump of her ankle had been neatly bandaged by Ojo, and when it was stripped showed a healing scar. The operator at Yanrin had even taken care to cut back the bone which was hidden in the flesh.

'Can you hear me, Aissa?' she asked again. 'Tell me where you're sick? Do you feel any pain?'

But Aissa lay silent, without a movement.

Hilda, seeing at last that Ojo was right, that she had to do with a sulky grief, the most intractable of native diseases, sighed and resigned herself to the loss of her night's sleep. She sat down on a broken mortar and lifted the girl's head into her lap. The head without its hair seemed absurdly small; it was very dirty, and the touch of its greasy skin sickened her nerves, but this feeling of disgust only increased her tenderness because she had been taught the logic of pity; that what is disgusting is by that the more pitiful.

She stroked the rough bristling skull and tried to console the girl. 'You mustn't grieve so, Aissa. You'll soon get your baby again. They wouldn't dare to kill a baby from the mission.'

Aissa did not answer or move. She heard the words, but they carried no meaning to her because she had done with life and everything and everybody in it.

Hilda understood her feelings very well. She pressed her in her arms like a hurt child.

'My poor Aissa, I know how angry you feel with everything, with us too who are trying to make you better.' (Hilda had never learnt anything about psychotherapy, which she supposed to be one of what her husband called these modern lickspittles to self-indulgence; but she knew the art, practised in every nursery since time beyond record, of curing a grief by describing it.) 'You don't want to be cured of your anger. You don't want that bad sorrow to be taken from you. You think that no one in the world has ever had such a big sorrow to bear. But do you know who had a much bigger sorrow, much worse pain?'

'It is Jesus, it is Jesus,' Ojo cried, carried away by the eloquence of his mistress; and the crowd sitting and kneeling behind, murmuring the name of Jesus, bowed like a cornfield.

'Yes, it is Jesus who suffered terrible pain to save us from the just punishment of our wickedness; and he suffers still when he sees us selfish and bad-hearted; angry over little things and obstinate in our poor little sorrows. I know how big your sorrow seems to you, Aissa, because I had a sorrow like that and I too was hard and wicked in my sorrow.'

Then she told how she too having lost her first baby by fever a year before, had been unhappy and angry for a long time; but how she had known all the time that her anger and sorrow were wicked because they opposed God's will who had permitted her baby to die. 'But one day when I thought of what Jesus had suffered for me I was ashamed of my bitterness, and I opened my heart to him. Then Jesus comforted me with his love so that I had never been so happy before.'

Hilda spoke well because she spoke to herself as well as to

147

Assia. She needed often to remind herself of her happiness and comfort in the love of Jesus.

'Now Jesus is closer to me than before. I know him better and love him better because I needed him and sought him in what I thought my great insupportable sorrow. That's what he meant when he said, "Blessed are they that mourn." For if there were no suffering in the world, no pain, no loss, no sin and anger, then we should not need the love of Jesus, we should not turn to him and trust him. We should never know the great love which changes the whole world and makes it into a kingdom of joy and peace, which gives so much happiness that the worst things that could happen to us seem just nothing at all and gives us understanding so that we can thank God for everything he has done.'

'Yes, yes, we very bad, we bad people,' Ojo murmured with the tears running down his cheeks.

Ojo, old Sara, Nagulo, the men and women crowding in the hut and the doorway, some sitting, some kneeling, were moved by Hilda's speech because it came from her heart. Some gazed at her open-mouthed, others, as if taken by shyness, at the door, but the more devout and practised like Ojo, who knew the right thing to do, knelt with downcast eyes and made little ejaculations of approval and sympathy.

Only Aissa had paid no attention; she had not even heard the words spoken to her; because her ears were closed, her brain was still without life. She was wholly given up to the bad spirit which filled her whole body like clay.

But suddenly old Sara, taking the opportunity of Hilda's first pause, began in a soft voice to croon the hymn: 'I am not worthy, Lord.'

The tune was taken up in a moment by a dozen voices, humming. Sara and Ojo, who alone knew some of the English version, murmured the words.

The rhythm played on Aissa, it poured through her body in

148

waves; it went through the bad spirit making him soft and weak, it washed him away like sand. The music took his place, it swayed and danced up and down through her head, her arms, her legs, her stomach, all her muscles, so that her head began to roll to and fro, her hands beat time, the notes came humming from her nose. At last her lips uttered the words:

'I am not worthy cold and bare
The lodging of my soul.'

They filled her throat, made the tears overflow from her eyes; she struggled to her knees and threw herself against the post of the hut, taking it in her arms, pressing her breasts against it so that the milk ran down, and cried out loudly: 'I shamed now, Jesus. You take me.'

They crowded round her laughing, exclaiming with delight. Ojo stammering with excitement embraced her: 'You come back, sister. You come to Jesus.'

Hilda, seeing the girl's hysterical excitement, sent away the crowd and caused Sara and another of the women to take her still weeping and praying to the native hospital. But another half hour passed before she grew more composed and, repeating often, 'I shamed now, Jesus, I shamed now,' she suddenly fell asleep.

It was now past five o'clock and there was barely light enough to distinguish the huts. But the broad surface of the Niger reflecting the stars and magnifying the false dawn threw up a faint moonstone radiance.

To Hilda this night view like a cathedral lit from below by votive candles accorded with feelings of joy and reverence. She did not need to thank God in words for the miracle of his goodness and mercy shown to the poor soul whom she had seen carried in one minute from misery and death to ecstasy; the whole being was thanks. It had been revealed to her once more what was the meaning of the grace of God which passes understanding, and she was filled with an extraordinary elation.

Staggering with fatigue and light-headed with sleeplessness she almost fell and put out her hand, which luckily touched the wall of a hut. She stood resting against the wall, and as she struggled for breath the crowing cocks in the boy's compound were like trumpets blowing for the triumph of her spirit. She wondered at her own excited happiness. How splendid life was to her compared with that of a poor blind worm like that red-faced district officer who had condescended to her last night; so pleased with himself, so pitiful in his ignorance and weakness, always in a fluster about his courts and his taxes, his trade and his roads, scuttling about like a rat in the dark; or of that silly girl who five years ago (it seemed a hundred to her surprised backward glance) had met the young Carr at a tea party and laughed at his solemn face and long pink nose. What a cold he had had. Lent time always gave him a cold. Even now he was pulled down. Because he was certainly far from well whatever he might say, and it was thoughtless of him to be worrying her to go home when he knew that he needed her. No doubt he would begin again at breakfast when he found out that she had been up these two hours. But if she did she would simply not answer. He was too stupid. Could he not see that she was anxious about him.

Hilda dragged herself heavily towards her house now already clear against the silver water. She was cold and her legs were aching. She sighed and reflected: 'I wonder will those roes be good still—he does so love roes for breakfast and I'm sure they have more vitamins in them than just fish.'

38 All rejoiced in Aissa's recovery and conversion; the members of the mission and even the people from the town crowded into the hospital all day, pleased even to look at the girl whom they regarded as a saint on account of her excitement and despair.

Hilda allowed these visitors, who brought presents and entered smiling with the most cheerful and admiring looks, because she thought that their attentions would distract Aissa; but in fact the girl scarcely looked at them, and did not notice anybody but Hilda herself, and Ojo, when they came to dress her leg or to encourage her.

'I shamed now,' she anxiously repeated the formula of her salvation; 'I no want nutting but Jesus.'

Hilda smiled and told her to be cheerful and go to sleep; but Ojo answered joyfully: 'Give all to Jesus, Aissa. Den he make you happy.'

'Yes, I give him all, Ojo. He make me happy.'

'You come with me, Aissa, we preach for Jesus in Kolu, we go burn dem juju house.'

But Aissa did not seem to hear this suggestion. At the notion of going back to Kolu again her whole body became weak with terror; she murmured faintly, weeping, 'I shamed now, I bad,' and she repeated like the child who says, 'I'm good now; I no want nutting but Jesus.'

At service the next morning she was placed in the front row. Hilda had dressed her in a clean white blouse and a striped blue skirt. Her short leg in a neat bandage stuck out in front of her, and she grasped in one hand a new crutch made by Carr himself.

The Carrs were delighted with the girl, for they saw that

she had attained to a true idea of religion and had in her some of the qualities of the saint. It was true that simplicity, confidence in faith, ecstasy, self-intoxication, were not uncommon among their converts; but that one which is the ground of all the rest, without which they are unfruitful, the power to continue in the same mood of devotion for some time and to return to it at will, was very rare indeed, so that they were as much pleased as surprised by Aissa's consistency in repentance.

It had been agreed that as she had finished her confirmation classes some time before she should receive communion this Sunday. The Carrs' object was to strengthen and comfort the girl in her new frame of mind, but the first result was to alarm her very much. She had even begged to be left out on the grounds of her unpreparedness, but Hilda smiled at her fears common among those taking communion for the first time, told her that she had nothing to be afraid of, and gave her a new scarlet and purple handkerchief for her cropped head. Every woman in the station envied Aissa this splendid head covering, but upon her it seemed to accentuate the dissipated, scared expression of her grotesque features. The girl seemed bewildered by her own emotions, and astonished to find herself the most popular person in Shibi. Her excitement and distress showed themselves as soon as the service began. She knelt in the wrong places, stood up when others were sitting, and several times broke into loud ejaculations and sobs. When the time came for the communicants to move forward she sank down on her knees and pretended not to see Mrs. Carr beckoning to her.

Hilda was obliged to come for her.

'Come, Aissa,' she said in her clear voice, for it was not her custom to whisper in that chapel which was hers as much as her husband's.

Aissa, turning up her round eyes like a frightened dog,

crouching down still further between the forms, muttered in terror: 'I no fit, ma—I no fit inside.'

'You needn't be afraid, Aissa. Only trust him and love him and he will give you his love. He will make you much happier than you can imagine.'

Aissa knew that Hilda was speaking what she knew to be true; her voice, her confident smile convinced her that great happiness was indeed within her reach. But she was terrified like a child before an operation. What would happen to her? What would it be like?

She tried to stammer that old formula which had given her comfort and softened her bitterness, 'I shamed, ma, I shamed,' but her great lips hung open so that she could not speak plainly, her leg bent under her, she fell on her knees at the palmwood rail and stooped her forehead almost to the ground.

She did not know what she was doing and she did not think. All her faculties were concentrated in fear and expectation. When Carr came to a stand in front of her she uttered a faint cry and struck her head on the rail.

Carr's voice murmured, 'The Body of our Lord'; her lips stretched forward in reproduction of the movement she had often seen made by the others; 'the Blood of our Lord'; she gulped the dark liquid in case it should choke her. She was startled by the taste; it was not like ordinary blood but sweet. In her surprise she did not notice that the others had gone back to their seats; nor in fact was she aware that Hilda and Shangoedi guided her to her own place and put her there on her knees. Her mind was wholly preoccupied. Her attention was all directed inwards to find out what was happening to her. What would Jesus do inside her? What would he feel like? What would he say? She perceived a faint warmth in her stomach. She brought all her mind upon the place. She held her breath. But the feeling had gone already. Where was it? She found it again deeper and further in. It grew quickly, it was like the morning sun whose rays grow stronger and warmer every minute; it pierced through the cold muscles; it passed outwards through the whole body in waves of heat burning out all her cold wickedness. It was making her like Jesus himself, pure so that she did not want Gajere any more, brave so that she was not afraid of the pagans, loving so that she loved Jesus with all her heart, happy so that she had never been so happy.

She was full of happiness. All that Mrs. Carr had promised her had come to pass. Gajere and Abba had vanished from her mind. All her anger and bitterness had gone. She was so happy that she wanted to laugh aloud, dance and sing.

She began to laugh, and finding herself on her knees in the midst of the congregation who were singing a Yoruba hymn, she sprang up and sang with them. She sang with such fervour that her voice gave a new tone to the whole volume of sound, and in her own ears it was as loud as a soldier's bugle and more beautiful than the agent's flute. She poured out her delight, her love:

'Oh Jesus, God and also man,
Who came to earth for love of us;
God of Gods, but born a baby,
Out of a virgin's womb.'

She fixed her eyes on the square of bright sky which could be seen through a large window hole above the altar and sang to Jesus in the sky hidden behind the veil of light.

'Oh what happiness to live for you,
Oh what joy to die for you,
Oh what joy of joys to see your face
For ever and ever.'

Shangoedi Ojo and Nagulo swayed to the music. Ojo was weeping as usual during hymns. His cracked voice made sounds like an animal in pain. Salé bellowed, grinning broadly,

154

his eyes closed in bliss. Nagulo was dancing in his place, his knees gave in turn, his large head rolled as if his neck were made of rubber, his shoulders and arms worked as if dragging up a net, his bloodshot eyes floated in brine, the foam ran down his little chin. Shangoedi uttered loud cries having no relation to the words or music; Aissa was carried away as if the music was lifting her body from the ground. She was so light with happiness that she could dance on air like a bird; she could sing like an angel, but even her beautiful voice and the beautiful words which expressed her happiness and love were not convincing enough for Jesus. She strove to make him believe; she stood on her toes to make him hear over Nagulo's rolling head which partly blocked the window; she used all the force of her lungs.

> 'Oh what happiness to live for you
> Oh what joy to die for you.'

The sky patch grew larger. Aissa was floating towards it. It dazzled her with its brightness and spread outwards until it was as large as the wall. Dark smudges appeared flashing here and there in its glittering depth, like fish; one larger than the rest waved more closely, stood still, darkened into a tall patch which came to the surface, and as it approached grew smaller and showed the face of a man with large eyes, a long nose, and a short beard like Umaru's.

Aissa recognized Jesus at once by his likeness to Umaru, who had often told her that he was a Jew and that Jews were a kind of Bedouin or Fulani. He belonged to her own tribe.

Jesus approached rapidly through the air breaking the light in front of him in two waves of glittering foam. His beauty surprised Aissa so much that she stood like a stick with her mouth open. He was a young man with a colour like her own and Umaru's, that of a lion's back; his long nose delicately formed, his mouth full and curved like a woman's, his eyes big and sparkling.

Aissa stretched out her arms to him, smiling and astonished with joy, and cried, 'Oh Jesus, my Jesus, my Jesus, you come for me.' She spoke English because she knew that it is God's language.

Jesus standing close to Aissa, but a little above her and just beyond her reach, smiled at her and said, 'You drink my blood, you belong to me now, Aissa.'

Aissa did not know how to express her gratitude, her devotion. 'Oh, Jesus, I love you too much, I love you too much. I belong for your woman. I do all ting to please you. You beat me, you kill me.'

To show her love she beat her breast with her fists. 'What I do for you, Jesus? I give you all myself. What I do for you?'

Aissa thought of what she could do for Jesus and at once she remembered that he had commanded Ojo to preach at Kolu. But at the notion of going to Kolu her legs became weak and her heart lay down.

Instantly Jesus said to her: 'You say you love me, Aissa, what, you go fight for me?'

Aissa did not reply.

Jesus said again in a sad voice: 'You go fight for me with dem bad pagan live for Kolu no love my Fader, no love me, bow down to Oke and juju gods.'

Aissa could not speak.

Jesus' face grew sad. He began to draw away, sighing: 'I see you fear too much dat Moshalo, dat Owule, dat Ajala. You fearful girl, Aissa. You no love me tall.'

But Aissa could not bear his reproachful look. She sprang towards him screaming in breathless haste: 'Yes I go, I die for you, I die for you. I go fight dem, I you girl, I die for you, my dear.'

156

The singing had stopped and everyone was gazing at the girl as she shouted towards the window. Hilda Carr touched her arm and asked her: 'What is it, Aissa, dear?'

Aissa stared at her with round eyes, her lips wet with bubbles of foam, and ejaculated: 'I see Jesus, ma. He come for me, he speak me.'

'But are you sure, Aissa?' She smiled and patted her arm. 'You know people think sometimes they see things—you must be careful—now wouldn't you like to come and lie down for a little?'

Carr, who had given the blessing, came up and his wife said with a wise smile: 'All this excitement has been a little too much for somebody.'

'Well, Aissa, what's it all about?' he asked her, smiling at the girl.

'Jesus come to me, Massa. He tell me be a good girl.'

'Well, I think now you *are* quite a good girl. Go easy with her, Hilda. It's like sleep-walking. They mustn't be wakened up too suddenly.'

Hilda showed her husband by a glance that she understood how to manage hysterical girls, and by a light shake of the head and pressure of her lips that she thought it unwise for him to discuss the case in front of the patient.

She led Aissa to her own verandah quickly to escape the crowd of mission men and boys pressing upon them, and asking, 'What is it?' Ojo, in great excitement, was shouting, 'You see Jesus, Aissa, you see Jesus—what he say you——?'

Shangoedi was shrieking Alleluia, and Umaru said often in his quiet voice: 'Shall we fight then? Is it the time?'

Aissa gazed at him with wide-open eyes, terrified, and said: 'I go fight dem, Jesus. I go fight dem.'

Hilda did not like to drive these people away for they were the most faithful and devoted of the congregation, but she hastened to take Aissa from them into her own room, where she made her lie down. She put her hand on the girl's forehead and said: 'Just rest there, dear. Close your eyes, and you'll soon feel better.'

Aissa sighed and closed her eyes. She lay still. Mrs. Carr, remembering a bromide medicine in her store room, ordered from Berua for Shangoedi's fits, went to make up a dose. But she had carcely turned before she heard a shout and saw Aissa on Nagulo's shoulder in the middle of an excited crowd, among whom she recognized Ojo, Umaru, Shangoedi and Kalé, running towards the town.

39 At the enquiry into the Yanrin riots it was suggested that both Bradgate and the Carrs had been negligent, the first in not arresting Ojo and Nagulo, and the second in making no attempt to prevent the raid. But the court agreed with the former that gaoling a fanatic is often more likely to start a riot than to prevent one, and Carr proved that it had been impossible to follow the raiders, or even to get news of them from Shibi, because Umaru seized all the boats and put a guard on the ferry.

MacEwen, who was president of the court, exonerated everybody; praised the Carrs for their magnificent work in Shibi, Bradgate for the notable progress of the last five years in Yanrin, the native administration for its statesmanlike coolness and moderation in a dangerous crisis.

Youngsters in the service called the report eyewash and MacEwen a time-server. Others, enemies of the mission, said that the sentimental old Scot had been affected by the sudden death, in painful circumstances, of Carr's wife, which occurred on the day before the enquiry opened.

But though MacEwen, like other men who had known her, admired Hilda Carr's goodness and sympathized with her husband, he was following his duty and not his feelings when he wrote his report. He was fair to everybody and considered the situation.

The Yanrin native government was not a very good one, but it was as good as Yanrin could provide for itself at that stage of development, and there was nothing to be gained by abusing it. In fact it is a rule of the service to do everything possible to support the prestige and self-confidence of native governments.

MacEwen did not write in the vein of a go-getter business expert seeking out inefficiency, but of a tactful friend encouraging a nervous household after some little domestic accident. His report was no more eyewash than common politeness. A child may be ugly and stupid, but it is stupid as well as cruel to say so. The ordinary person praises it for what he can find to praise, and afterwards, if he likes, he can recommend a tutor or a specialist.

MacEwen did in fact recommend for Yanrin on Bradgate's strong request an increased vote for education, and for roads, bridges and markets, and the Treasury allowed one-quarter of his minimum figure. Next year five pupils from Yanrin went to learn football, cricket and the multiplication tables at Berua government school. At the same time two missions have set up rival camps and schools, the Original Apocalypse at Ketemfe, who preach the full Bible and the end of the world in five years, and the Mennonites at Yanrin. They have about sixty eager learners. There is going to be a steel bridge at Akoko.

40 Old Musa in Kolu nearly prevented the riot at its very beginning. About nine o'clock when he first heard of the landing of the Christians he put on his best turban, called his two men, and trotted at once to the market place, where he found two hundred people in front of Obasa's house. They were dancing, shouting, chasing each other and laughing at the Christian women, especially Shangoedi, who was rushing up and down flourishing two knives and screaming, 'Fight for Jesus.'

Aditutu the midwife had joined them; she was already drunk, and though she shouted the Christian war cry she was also making fun of it.

Musa flew at the mob with such ferocity of gesture and voice that he scattered it and almost made it run. But Shangoedi and Aditutu caught him by a trick. They crawled to his feet shouting for mercy, then Aditutu jumped up and seized him round the body, holding his arms, and Shangoedi cut his throat so quickly and dexterously that his voice was stopped in the middle of a word.

The crowd, seeing this feat, ran back and took their revenge on Musa's body and also on the constables, whom they beat and trampled to death. Since Obasa was in prison there was now no guardian of the peace in Kolu, and in half an hour the town was burning in a dozen places. Every house was sacked.

In a very short time the news reached Shibi and the islands as well as every part of Yanrin that the Christians had declared a holy war and sacked Kolu. All the blackguards, the starving, the out of works, the boys who had never known a real war, the waterside aliens, the women from the brothels, not only in Yanrin Emirate but from twenty miles outside its borders, hurried to see the fun, to take their part in it, preferably on the stronger side, and to pick up what they could.

41 The first news of the riot was brought to Yanrin by a girl from Kolu who was overheard shouting to a friend across the street. Being taken up by a policeman and brought to the palace, very much ashamed and overcome by shyness, she whispered to Mallam Adamu that the Christians had killed duckfeet (Musa) and that Umaru the Christian was talking to the people; he promised them rain if they would follow him, and he said that any who were killed would go straight to the Christian paradise where they would have for their wives white girls with wings. He had a picture of these girls. Their wings were like stork's wings. All the young men had followed him to Ketemfe. He was a very tall, fierce man, a Fulah.

Mallam Adamu would not believe this nonsense, and returned at once to his afternoon nap. The Emir and his secretary Illo had not been waked from theirs. Thus when Nagulo and Ladije (a local bully and friend of Nagulo's) arrived in the market place with their followers, they met no opposition at all and mastered the town, except the palace, in half an hour.

They broke open the gaol and let out the prisoners who at once murdered the Alkali. Waziri was dragged into the palace covered with bruises and wounds. Clerk Williams was also chased to cover and his house burnt.

Afterwards the Emir and his councillors were greatly praised for their moderation in allowing without protest three prison warders and a score or two of Yorubas and Ejaws, men, women and children, to be hacked to pieces. But in fact they were taken by surprise in the first place, and afterwards being summoned in council they could not decide on a common policy.

161

Zeggi and Yerima wanted to shoot at the mob, which was at that moment flogging several traders to death in full view of the palace walls, but Mallam Isa, a district judge, who hoped to succeed the Alkali in his post, declared that it would be stupid to use guns, first because the judge did not know that the Emir had any other guns than the ones used for salutes, and to shoot them would betray the fact; secondly because, according to white man's law, it was unlawful to shoot at a mob until either a government policeman or soldier had been killed.

'But we'll say that we thought that one of them was killed.'

The Emir, who had sat on his carpet throughout these discussions with folded hands and a look of dignity, saying nothing, since he did not care to expose himself to contradiction and shame, now was observed to shake his head: 'Whatever we do, we shall be blamed.'

'Send to the judge,' cried Mallam Isa, 'that is the only safe course.' For Mallam Isa was determined not to do anything offensive to Bradgate.

'But meanwhile the blackguards will destroy us.'

'That won't be our fault however,' cried the Mallam.

'Nevertheless we shall suffer,' said the Emir.

'That's certain,' said old Mallam Yacubu, 'for when the Emir of Berua and all his officers and his household were murdered by the Berua pagans the judge said that it was their own fault because they had offended the pagans. He praised the pagans and asked their advice about choosing a new emir.'

'True,' said the Emir, 'for the judges don't care if we are all killed. They care only to please the people, who are the stronger.'

42 The Council was sitting in the great hall of the palace, a high whitewashed room surrounded by pillars of red and white mud. It was windowless except for a few slits near the ceiling, thirty feet up and full of bird's nests, so that the noise of the mob reached the elders only as a murmur like that of the wind in a wood. It was not loud enough to oblige the Emir or Mallam Yacubu to raise their voices, and so they did not mind it very much. As for danger they minded that rather less, for they were both convinced that youth in paradise was preferable to old age in modern Yanrin. At this time when it was already dark in the hall, an old ragged slave came from behind the pillars which sheltered a crowd of refugees, squatting in silence among their boxes and bundles, and announced to the Emir that Mallam Ali had come.

The Emir showed no sign of hearing the statement. It was not etiquette for him to receive it from such a person. It was only when Mallam Adamu, chief in rank of those present, had repeated to him that he sighed. 'What Ali is this?'

'What Ali is this?' Adamu enquired.

'Lord, Ali dan Waziri.'

He turned again to the Emir. 'King of the world, it is Ali, son of Waziri.'

'If he has news, bring him in.'

Ali was standing in full view close behind his announcer. He had grown thin and his expression was alarmed, but he was wearing a new gown and a new sword with red curtain tassels nine inches long.

At Mallam Adamu's signal he assumed a haughty expression and approached with a deportment which seemed like a caricature of the Emir's own royal gait; the slow rolling steps of a great chief encumbered by half a dozen robes, horse boots and trailing slippers over the boots.

Falling on his knees he saluted the Emir and said, 'I come to serve you, Lord.'

'The Emir thanks you,' said Mallam Adamu. 'What is the news?'

'The news is that the Christians have attacked the juju house at Ketemfe, but the devils in the wood caught Umaru who was their leader and killed him. Then the others ran away.'

This gave great satisfaction. Everyone but the Emir showed his pleasure. He murmured a question.

'And this woman Aissa and the Yoruba Ojo, where are they?'

'Aissa is at Kolu with the women. Ojo is at Ketemfe seeking to gather his people again. But if you give me leave and two men I propose to catch him.'

The Emir spoke to Mallam Adamu, who turned again to Ali. 'My lord says that this would be a good act but difficult.'

It was obvious that the boy was in that excited condition of young people who play a grand part without much regard to what they are undertaking. His fingers were trembling and he was obliged several times to wet his lips with his tongue. But the councillors were pleased with his loyalty and courage; even Yerima grunted approval.

'But how will he do it?' the Emir asked.

'How will you do it?' said Mallam Adamu.

'I shall go by the stable drain and the water gate. Then to Ketemfe by bush tracks. There I shall come upon them suddenly and arrest Ojo. I shall return by Kolu and take Aissa on the way.'

'There are a great many of them.'

'Not so many as there were in Kolu on Oke's day.'

164

'That time you succeeded, this time you may fail and then they will kill you.'

'What of that?' said the boy with a wave of his hand; and this brag, which was perfectly sincere (what did Ali care for death at this glorious moment), made a bad impression.

'You do not mind danger then?' said Yerima, with a sly glance at Mallam Isa.

'The more danger the more honour,' said Ali carelessly. But he had been turning over this phrase for a long time, and he was glad to have the opportunity of using it.

All were offended by the boy's conceited airs which he had assumed to gain their respect and to play his part like a man.

Yerima uttered a rude laugh, the others more polite made no outward sign of their desire to teach the youth what was the right thing. The Emir said in his tired voice, 'If he thinks he can succeed he can try, but he must not get into trouble, or hurt anybody belonging to the white man at Shibi.'

'Or shoot anybody,' said Mallam Isa.

Ali bowed low. 'I shall take care of that, Lord. Rely upon me. I thank you. I go.'

He rose and strutted away with even more dignity than before; because he was disappointed. He had expected praise, admiration. But he knew from his lessons at football that a desire for these must not be confessed even to oneself. He put his disappointment from him and did not feel it. He felt more lonely, responsible, majestic; so that he threw his legs higher and wider; he carried himself like the greatest of chiefs, and the deportment of his body became that of his spirit. He felt like a great chief, and the respect which the councillors would not give he gave himself.

He did not notice that he had been set difficult conditions because his mind was fixed upon glory and not on success.

165

43 Zeggi was pleased with Ali, congratulated him and gave him much good advice. Also he handed over to him the two men Dan Angass and Suli. Dan Angass like Zeggi was a veteran, an old soldier of the Niger Company; a little pagan, middle-aged, with a bald head and broken teeth. He was grumbling: 'So we're going on this fool's game. What, is this boy going to take us? Then we're done for.'

'What matter!' said the other. 'We are done for anyhow.' Suli was from Berua, a large powerful rascal contemptuous of all the Yanrin tribes.

Zeggi made these two take off their red gowns and turbans so that they appeared like private citizens. Ali had no disguise. All three hid their mouths in their turbans.

Zeggi conducted them through the postern and pointed out from there a way by the ruins of Waziri's house towards the water gate. He then shook hands with Ali, assumed an important serious expression like that of a corporal congratulating a hero, and said in English, 'All right, you good man.'

Ali, much encouraged by this compliment, led his men through the broken houses towards the gate, a narrow hole in the wall through which in the wet season a small banana swamp drained into the river. This drain or brook was now dried up. But when they came close to the gate they found that a house nearby was on fire and surrounded by a crowd of islanders; they had to change their plans, and ascended the wall, which on the inside had a gradual slope. As they had feared this exposed them from a distance. The islanders saw Ali on the wall when he rose into the firelight, and one of them shouted: 'Hail Ali, great chief, friend of the Emir of Kano.'

This caused a yell of laughter which annoyed Dan Angass,

who answered, 'Silence, you dogs, your manners are shameful.'

Ali, offended by the chaff, told the man to hurry up, but Dan Angass grumbled for a long time. 'This is a nice business, to get killed for nothing. A pound a month—it isn't worth it. My God, it isn't—No, no, Dan Angass, you're a fool to be here. I'm going home, I say.'

Ali paid no attention to the man's grumbles because Zeggi had said to him: 'You can trust Dan Angass. Even alone, he will do what he has to do. Suli is braver, but do not let him be frightened or he'll run off.'

Ketemfe is twelve miles from Yanrin and lies in a large peninsula of which two sides are formed by a loop of the Niger and the Ketemfe river; the third, or neck, is chiefly a swamp. The rear end is covered by thick bush hiding two small villages as well as Owule's, which is close to the second grove in the farthest angle of the promontory.

Ali and his two men travelling in the bush along cattle tracks parallel with the road, to avoid being seen, reached the swamp, which was dry and cracked, in three hours. Half a mile further on the narrow bush track expanded into a broad clearing in front of the grove; a space of hard beaten clay sloping gently on two flanks to the Niger and Ketemfe. On the far side the roofs and granaries of the village could be seen like a row of saw teeth black against the bright steel colour of the Niger. Owule's huts were out of sight. They lay behind the grove. The moon was still high enough to light the two rivers, the wall-like front of the grove and the whole clearing which was crowded with people sitting and standing in groups, all the men armed and many of the women carrying loads. Most of these were silent or spoke in such low tones as could not be heard above the yells of drinkers or the voices of several speakers who were exhorting them.

Ali had not expected to see so many people among whom it

would be difficult to find the leaders. He stood watching the groups, which were in slow movement, and trying to decide what to do next.

The mob grew thicker towards the grove and a shrill voice could be heard crying: 'What are you afraid of—do you want to die of starvation—Owule, what is Owule, I tell you he is no good—what, a weak old man—nothing—you kill him, the rain come, then God send you good things.'

Ali turned towards this voice and immediately Suli, seeing him decided, thrust before him and struck out right and left with his spear shaft, roaring, 'Make way, you scum—make way.' The people hastily threw themselves out of the path and Ojo's voice faltered. He turned and seeing Ali coming towards him with the two dogarai broke off his speech and stood with open mouth and staring eyes.

'What do you want?' he shouted.

Ali did not answer him. He would not condescend to speak to the fool.

'Don't you touch me,' Ojo shouted. 'I curse you—God curse you.'

A woman's voice from the crowd called out, 'Ali is our friend, you needn't be afraid.'

Suli with a menacing flourish of his spear shouted at them: 'Salute you dogs, salute our great lord, salute Ali dan Waziri, the friend of Bradgate.'

Many of the people in front fell on their knees and cried loudly, 'Hail, Lord, pardon Lord.'

Ali waved his hand towards Ojo and said, 'Tie him up.'

Dan Angass threw a loop of rope over Ojo's head who, when he felt it, uttered a scream of terror and struggled like a rabbit in a net, 'Let me go, I curse you, let me go.'

Dan Angass gave the rope a twist cutting off the prisoner's breath and said to him, 'Now then, keep still—as if our troubles weren't enough.' He jerked the boy off his feet, and then with

168

an expert twist of the rope, caught up his right hand and tied it to his neck.

Ali turned to the people and said severely: 'What have you been doing, you foolish ones? Do you then think it is a good thing to burn houses and steal? Are you not afraid of punishment?'

The audience began to press back from him in alarm. Many unable to escape fell on their knees and salaamed murmuring, 'Pardon, pardon.'

A voice cried out, 'We were only watching, master. It was Nagulo burnt the houses.'

'I know that and Nagulo will be condemned. But you also are guilty for not preventing these wicked acts. That is the law. Go home now, at once. Be off.'

Suli echoing this 'Be off' in a bellow, rushed forward with his spear, whereupon the whole crowd turned tail, falling over each other in their hurry and screaming with panic. However, they could not go far on that side, which was full of holes and thorn bush, and when they broke in the other direction they were cut off by another large party advancing by the road. This party now struck up a hymn.

Suli, whose ears and eyes were extremely sharp, said to Ali: 'It's the people from Kolu with the witch. We'd better get off while we can.'

'Which way are they going—to the juju grove?'

'Yes, the juju grove no doubt.'

'Then we had better get there before them. Which is the road?'

'Yes, yes, master. This way, this way,' said Suli in a fluster.

'I say nothing,' Dan Angass growled, giving Ojo's rope a shake, 'but that's not the path to the grove. It's over there. If we wanted to stop these sons of bitches we should go there by the kuka tree, right in the eye of the path.'

169

Ali saw at once that Suli had been trying to mislead him, and said to Angass: 'That's our way. Suli can go home if he likes.'

Suli began to bluster, swearing that he would slaughter any man who called him a coward, but the others turned their backs upon him and walked off.

Dan Angass, whose professional habit of mind had thus condemned him in a desperate situation, now began to protest as if to the air: 'I didn't say it was good for us to be there. But I can see this young bighead wants us to be killed. That's not my business I suppose. Come on then you booby' (to Ojo, with a jerk at the rope), 'who cares what happens to Dan Angass,' and grumbling at every step he led the way to a position in the mouth of the grove which commanded the passage.

'There,' he said, 'this is the proper place for the business as any fool ought to see.'

'Yes, it's a good place,' Ali said, speaking with the coolness appropriate of an army commander. But he was not quite satisfied with his intonation and therefore repeated in a different rhythm with a gesture added (carelessly throwing back his sleeve over his shoulder), 'It will do well.'

Ali was in fact perfectly cool because he was too closely preoccupied with his management of the enterprise and his own conduct to notice danger. Dan Angass' prophecies, which grew more and more gloomy, and the terrified countenance of Suli who now came sidling up to rejoin his comrade, had no effect upon him. He took his stand directly in the mouth of the path which disappeared behind him into a cave of foliage like a tunnel.

44 The Kolu party having advanced to within fifty yards struck up their war song which they yelled, some in Hausa, some in Yoruba, mixed with cries of hate and adoration.

'Forward, soldiers of Jesus,
Marching to the war,
With the cross for our flag
Carried before you.'

Aissa carried on Aditutu's shoulders headed the column and was singing in English. Her eyes were closed. She beat the time with her hand and her voice overbore all the rest. Ali stepped forward and raised his hand.

Suli shouted in a terrible voice, 'Stop, stop!'

Aditutu bending beneath her load and intoxicated with beer and music did not see Ali; she did not come to a halt until Suli struck her in the breast with the butt of his spear. She staggered and fell. Aissa, silenced as if by a bullet, rolled kicking on the ground. The column split and hesitated.

Those behind continued to sing, but Ali's voice was clearly heard by the front ranks when he commanded Aissa to be tied.

Dan Angass advanced, pushed a woman out of his way, and threw a rope over Aissa's head, saying, 'Lie still, you silly woman or you'll hurt yourself.'

Aissa struggled to her knees and looked at them in amazement. She did not know where she was or what had happened. But suddenly she saw the grove in front of her, and falling on her face tried to crawl aside, crying in terror, 'Jesus, Jesus!'

Ali stepped forward and waved his hand, the crowd separated, the hymn wavered and stopped. He cried in his shrill voice, 'Off with you—you fools, or it will be the worse for you. Go now, run.'

171

A voice cried, 'It is Ali.'

'Ali is our friend, it was he who saved our lady from Obasa.'

Ali, glad to explain the truth to these ignorant people, shouted, 'I saved you from Obasa because he had no right to hurt you, but neither have you any right to injure Owule. So go now—I warn you.'

Old Sara, who stood in the front row, looked at him through her gold spectacles with the air of superior knowledge and said: 'Zaki, you do not understand. Owule is a devil. He worships a false god, and because of that the true god gives us no rain. The people are dying because of Owule.'

The boy answered with contempt, speaking loudly in order to be heard: 'This is a silly tale. No one can make rain. It falls when the clouds are ripe, and if Owule has done wrong then he must be taken to the court and tried. That is the law and besides it is right as anyone can see.'

Meanwhile the section at the tail of the column led by Shangoedi, finding their course stopped, were calling out to know what had happened. They broke through the front row of the men and at once the lunatic screamed, 'They've caught Aissa.'

Shangoedi and the rearguard rushed forward flourishing knives and clubs. The guardsmen raised their spears and Ali his hand as if to forbid the approach of these people. He assumed a more haughty expression and looked angrily at them.

But Shangoedi hated Ali as a traitor. It was fixed in her head that he had betrayed the Christians in Kolu. When she saw him in front of her she uttered a scream of rage and, careless of the spear points, flew at him. She twisted under the spears in a flash, threw Ali down and struck at him with her knife, cutting open his breast to the bone. Suli had dropped his spear and run off. Dan Angass hit Shangoedi with the butt of his spear in the forehead, knocking her senseless. He exclaimed

172

angrily to Ali on the ground, 'There you are. I told you so,' but at this instant he was killed by a thrown matchet which struck him in the throat.

Ali overrun by the charge could not be found. But Makoto, who was one of those rescued from prison, was shouting, 'Where is Ali? Catch him!' and one of the bystanders, a young Kolua boy, anxious to be useful to the great man, ran here and there, and soon with his quick attentive eyes made out something like an animal moving on all fours in the bush at the edge of the grove. He darted into the bush and saw that this was Ali creeping away. He looked up and begged in a low voice, 'Don't tell them—don't tell them.'

But the child, overjoyed by the discovery and his usefulness, had not time to listen to what he was saying. He flew back into the road to seek Makoto, crying, 'Here he is—I found him.' Makoto had gone on with the other Christian leaders headed by Aissa on Aditutu's back. She had struck up again the war song and the little band of Christians behind her, possessed by the words which they wailed in long swelling notes, could not hear the boy's voice. He was entangled with the laughing holiday crowd from the riverside at Kolu; young boatmen, traders and their local girls come to see the show.

Some of these heard the boy and two big Nupe bargemen asked, 'Who is it?' The boy caught one of them by the leg, 'Quick, quick, this way—it's Ali.'

'What Ali?'

'He tried to kill Aissa, the holy one, the priestess of Jesus. He's just in here behind the thin bush.'

Ali jumped up to run, but immediately a dozen voices shouted, 'Catch him.' The Nupes had already pounced upon him and held him by the arms.

'Well, what shall we do with him?'

'Who is he? Who are you, boy?'

A woman's voice from the crowd called out, 'That's Ali, the Waziri's son.'

'Are you Ali? Here, speak, or we'll teach you.'

'I am Ali dan Waziri, and you'd better let me go.'

One of the women in the crowd said, 'Hear him, what a swell!' and uttered a shriek of laughter, causing everyone to laugh.

Ali was frightened and could not control his trembling muscles. Looking round at the laughing crowd he recognized Jacob, and exclaimed in English, 'Jacob, you tell them to let me go.'

Jacob, making comical faces, repeated, 'I tellum let you go!' and uttered another loud guffaw, 'Whoffer I do that?'

'You're my friend, Jacob.'

Jacob, in great indignation, shouted: 'Me. I no be your friend. I no be frien for Waziri. I no gree for kings not nutting. You tink yourself better dan somebody. Whoffer peoples born de same. Jesus say all big men's, all rich people, go to hell. I gree for Jesus.'

Pleased with this argument he repeated it in Yoruba to the crowd of whom several shouted: 'That's it—that's it—no more rich.' But they spoke in a good-humoured fashion and continued to laugh. Jacob strutted away with his hat on the side of his head. He was delighted with himself for hitting the right popular note.

'What shall we do with him?' the Nupes asked the others.

'Take me to my father and he will reward you,' Ali said.

'Ah! but suppose the Christians cut his throat.'

One of the women eager to make another joke, cried, 'Your father—the Christians are going to make meat of him.'

Ali recognized a tall ferryman who had often poled him across the Niger, the most good-natured of men. He started forward and caught the fellow's loin-cloth: 'Adamu, you won't let them kill me?'

The fellow, embarrassed, smiled at the crowd, and answered, 'Well, it's not my business, you see.'

'But my father——'

'Yes, but things may be a bit different. Suppose they cut his throat.

'But when the white man comes with the soldiers——'

'Yes, when?' cried one of the women, and another remarked: 'Even if he does he can't do anything to us. He won't bother about people like us.'

Now a friend of the Nupes came up, a big, stout, kindly woman, smiling broadly. They saluted her warmly, she them, and being asked her opinion she advised them to tie Ali up in a safe place till the battle was decided. Then they could sell him to the winning side. 'If the Emir wins Waziri will give you a present for saving his life, and if the Christians win they will want him for a prisoner.' She laughed in satisfaction of her good reasoning.

Ali fell suddenly on his knees and caught the Nupe woman by the hand: 'Make them take me home—make them take me home.'

The woman was surprised and embarrassed—she tried to disengage the boy's fingers, laughing and saying to the bystanders: 'Well, that's right, isn't it? I've got to do what's the best thing for my friends.'

Many voices from the crowd approved her: 'That's right. Of course you have. That's good advice.'

45 The second attack of the Christians on the juju grove was led by Makoto, a Shibi farmer called Ladije, Ojo, with Dan Angass's rope still hanging down his back, and behind them Aissa, who was singing louder and louder in order to frighten the devils.

Ojo in front, his eyes bulging, the sweat pouring down his face, was shrieking defiance into the dark cave among the trees: 'You look out, you black debbil, you better look out. Jesus is coming. Ah, you fear now, you done for, you damn bad debbil. Run away quick.'

He shook his fists at the devil and yelled, 'Run now, quick. I tell you, Jesus is coming,' and he made as if to rush into the grove. But though his legs worked up and down like pistons he did not move forward.

Ladije and Makoto also failed to advance. The enchantment had already caught their feet, and Makoto moaned, 'Ah! it's medicine, it's medicine.'

But the column behind led by Shangoedi and Aissa surged forward and drove the men before them. Shangoedi, whose eye had been knocked out and whose face streamed with blood, danced against them, kicking them with her knees and yelling in chorus with Aissa close behind

'Forward Jesus soldiers,
To the holy war.'

The whole column, packed close together, drove through the dark tunnel under the trees like a jet of steam.

Owule and his family were taken by surprise. They had not expected another charge so soon. The eldest son and chief fighting man had gone to Yanrin for help, only Adikunle the youngest, aged sixteen, and two male pupils not much older, were on watch.

Adikunle, whose duty it was to guard the path, struck at the Christian leaders with a club. But in his terror he did not take good aim and hit Ojo a glancing blow on the skull. Makoto instantly disembowelled him with an upward cut with his matchet. He, feeling his responsibility discharged, crawled back to the juju house, and while he was lying against his mother's knees surrounded by the weeping women and screaming babies, old Owule in a palsy of fright put himself inside the tall framework of the juju dress and stood at the door. He prayed aloud with all the force of his lungs to Shango, Ifa and Oke to protect him from his enemies, reminding them that they were the enemies also of the old and true religion.

Meanwhile the leaders of the attacking column, driven forward by those behind, stumbling over roots and running into trees at every corner of the winding track, had suddenly reached the clearing. Here the path widened like a river at its mouth so that the front ranks were able to spread out, the pressure was released, and all came to a halt. Their shouts ceased, even Aissa's voice faltered into silence. The clearing was about thirty yards long and fifteen yards wide. Most of the ground was covered with thick undergrowth, tufts of burnt grass, tree stumps, but the juju house with a tumble-down roof stood by itself on an irregular patch of bare earth. Clearing and hut were brilliantly illuminated by the moon, so that the rough grass, tree stumps, and the hut appeared dead white with black shadows. The bare smooth ground on which the hut stood glistened like starched cloth.

Nothing moved, nothing could be heard, and the Christians, standing open-mouthed from their defiant shouts, gazed as if struck by the same enchantment which had stiffened the grass into motionless wire and fixed the shadows like paint.

Owule, as frightened as Ladije and the rest but more desperate, stepped from the juju house into the moonlight, and at sight of this figure, nine feet high, with a gleaming white

177

face more than three feet long, Ladije and Makoto dropped their spears.

Owule speaking into the wooden megaphone formed within his mask began to utter Oke's curse upon her enemies. The Christians turned and ran. But they did not utter a sound. Nothing was heard except the sudden rush of their hard feet upon the earth and the thuds, cracks and rattles of their falling weapons as they battered themselves on the trees or tripping in thorns, fell heavily against the ground and each other.

46 When Aditutu tried to run away she fell over her own feet and threw Aissa into the bush. Aissa had but a glimpse of the devil before she stopped singing. Then she closed her eyes and began to pray. When she found herself on the ground she crawled into the bush. But all this time she was full of the spirit of Jesus. She felt him in every part of her like strong beer making her heart beat furiously with the courage of a warrior, her brain hot with bold glorious thoughts, and all her muscles jump with energy and joy.

As soon therefore as she began to creep away this spirit speaking in her head said in a tone of great surprise, 'You no run away, Aissa.'

Aissa did not answer but still tried to push her way into the thick scrub. Then the spirit said again with astonishment, 'You fraid, Aissa? You no belong for Jesus no mo, Aissa? How you do then? Jesus inside you now. He speak to you.'

Aissa was confused. There was no doubt about Jesus being inside her. She felt him still to the very ends of her fingers and toes; he was still throbbing like a warrior in her heart, tingling like joy in her hands and forehead, filling her brain with songs and visions of Mrs. Carr, angels, Abba, Gajere, huge pots of beer and bowls of corn, bright new cloths in all the newest stripes and the broad smiles of friends. He was there and he was speaking to her, but she, Aissa, was crawling away. Aissa was a disobedient girl, a very bad girl. Look at the way she was behaving to Jesus who loved her. How could she expect to go to heaven and see Abba and Gajere again?

She abused herself. 'You bad girl, Aissa,' joining in with the spirit who was saying indignantly, 'You no love me tall, Aissa.'

Aissa was confused and ashamed, but she did not try to defend herself. She wanted to hide and she continued to crawl among the tree trunks, wriggling beneath the creepers, turning here and there to find an opening.

Suddenly she found herself at the edge of the grove and saw the juju house in front of her and much closer than before. Ojo was beside her, his face twisted with fear. He caught hold of her and began to sing or rather whisper through his chattering teeth the Yoruba hymn

> 'Let us stand below the cross
> So that the blood from His side
> May fall on us drop by drop.'

The tall devil made another step forward, his long steel teeth, as large as cooks' knives, parted widely, flashing in the moonlight.

Aissa felt weak, she was sinking down. She clung to Ojo and sighed the words of the hymn

> 'Jesus for us was put to death.'

Her voice murmuring these words made her strong with their strong medicine. She felt Jesus springing and dancing within her, she triumphed over that bad Aissa, whose legs had tried to crawl away. She drew herself up and sang loudly, defying the devil

> 'A broken heart, a sea of tears:
> These we bring.'

179

The magic words sung in Aissa's and Ojo's quavering voices made Owule's legs shake. The giant devil quivered from head to foot; its great eyes rolled and its iron teeth clashed together. Aissa uttered a loud cry.

'Oh, Jesus, I die for your love. I die for you'; she stretched out her arms.

Ojo put a matchet in her hand and said: 'You holy girl, Aissa, you kill the devil now.' Aissa's fingers closed on the matchet; she tried to answer that she would kill the devil, but no word came. Ojo thrust his head between her legs, lifted her up, staggered forward. Owule drooping with fear leant towards them and Aissa struck at the huge white face and glittering eyes, as big as plates, with her matchet, but could not reach it.

Owule tried to turn aside and avoid the blow, but the unwieldy dress swung and caught his feet. Aissa rolled off Ojo's shoulders, and as she fell almost fainting against the white face she struck at it a second time with her matchet. It fell and she fell beside of it. With yells of triumph the Christians who had watched the duel from the edges of the grove rushed forward. Someone with a torch lit the juju frame of plaited grass and cloth and the whole burst into flames. Owule uttered loud screams within and kicked his legs through the grass, but Ladije and Makoto held him down with their spears.

Aissa, rolling on the ground with shut eyes, bewildered, crying out, 'No, no, no,' to the devil whom she expected every moment to tear her flesh, was lifted up screaming and found herself surrounded by a yelling laughing crowd who jostled each other to salute her. They carried her into Owule's house and put her in his chair, caressed her, offered her beer, calabashes full of shell money from the juju house. Someone placed Abba in her lap. He had been found among Owule's women, fat and well. They had fattened him to die, but they had not yet dared to kill him. He stared at his mother with a bored, absent-minded expression while she held him up, uttering shrill shrieks of joy like the notes of a parakeet. She rolled in the chair and tossed him in her arms: 'You see,' she screamed at the crowd, which imitated her cries and even her expression of joyful excitement: 'You see, Jesus give him back. Jesus pleased with me. He gree for me now, Jesus, he ma frien now.'

'You kill de debbil, Aissa,' they cried at her. 'You kill de debbil for Jesus.'

'Yes, I killum. De holy gote run after me, he tell me, you bad girl, Aissa, you fear too much. Den I call for Jesus, I killum.'

'You give us de rain now, Aissa.'

'Yes, I give you de rain, I give you de Kingdom of Heaven.' She looked round at them proudly. But suddenly a loud neigh of laughter was heard. Gajere came thrusting through the women.

Aissa as soon as she set eyes on Gajere also burst out laughing. Everybody in the house began to laugh. They pushed Gajere towards Aissa, then ran out of the house pushing each other, shrieking with laughter. Gajere was left bowing towards his wife with loud guffaws and looking slily at her while she bent towards him and laughed so much that she wept.

47 Ojo and his party went directly from Ketemfe to Yanrin, but a great many of the farmers who had joined him from Kolu and the Ketemfe neighbourhood hurried straight home to prepare their ground for the rain, which was expected at once according to the prophecy. 'Owule fell and the rain fell.'

Ojo, when he got to Yanrin, at once proclaimed the Kingdom of Heaven and gave out the following orders, of which the Hausa version, written by a tax mallam in Latin characters, was afterwards sent to the Governor as a curiosity:

'No one is to have or keep any property which is abolished.

'No one is to use money which is abolished.

'No one is allowed to marry as fornication is forbidden.

'It is forbidden to drink beer, gin, whisky.

'All judges are abolished including the white judges. Only God is judge. All laws are abolished except the law of God written in His book.

'All books are to be destroyed except God's book.

'Those who do not become Christians are to be killed, and the white men who are not Christians shall be driven away.'

The paper was headed: 'In the name of Jesus and the Holy Spirit, orders for the Kingdom of Heaven, by Ojo, servant of God.'

At this time, about ten in the morning, the police detachment sent off from Berua at dawn in two lorries was still thirty miles from Shibi, and the Carrs had only just begun to understand that the fires in Kolu which had brightened the sky all night were connected with the mysterious absence of three-quarters of their converts.

In Yanrin the whole town was on fire and the front wall of the palace had been breached by a digging party, chiefly of women, under the fearless Shangoedi.

Ojo and his followers' belief that God had decreed the end of the emirates and the empire was not surprising, especially when it is considered that thousands of persons anxious to become Christians at once were crowding round them wherever they went, falling at their feet, shouting salutations; and that up to this moment they had suffered only two casualties, Umaru and a woman called Ada shot by Zeggi under the palace wall; while the enemies of Jesus (as Ojo called them) had been killed by dozens, from the Alkali, the prison warders, Owule and his family, Musa, Moshalo, and numerous other priests, some killed by their own villagers, to Zeggi, who was hacked to pieces by the women in the breach, which he alone, at the first collapse of the wall, dared to defend.

In fact the few guards who had been in the palace at the first outbreak, or who had escaped there from the Treasury and the prison, amounting to about a dozen, and the servants, refugees and domestic slaves who formed the palace garrison, were demoralized by the report that everywhere in Nigeria the Christians, made impregnable by their magic, had driven out the Emirs, white judges, and even the soldiers and police.

This news, which was believed by most of the Christians also, was shouted triumphantly at the palace by the new converts who, wearing a page of the Bible slung from their necks by a string laughed and made rude gestures when they were fired at; and it was confirmed by the failure of the Yanrin police detachment to come to the rescue of the government.

Half a dozen messengers had been sent to the barracks during the night, but neither they nor the police had returned.

In this desperate strait the guards had been permitted to use their guns, but they did not hit anybody with them, partly on account of the difficulty of hitting anything with a dane gun at a range of more than ten yards and partly because they did not take aim. What was the good of aiming at persons whose bodies had been rendered invulnerable?

It should be said that many of the magical paper breast plates afterwards found on prisoners proved to be made of newspapers, and even some of Bradgate's novels were torn up and sold by speculators among whom Jacob was one of the most successful. But they fulfilled their purpose at that time in giving Ojo's newest disciples the courage of tigers who also do not expect to be killed; and in filling the palace garrison with despair.

At the very sight of Shangoedi, stark naked, with her broken eye, her face masked in a brown coat of dried blood, crosses slung from her neck and tied to each arm, a huge knife in her hand, rushing and leaping to the attack with shrieks of: 'Jesus, Jesus, kill them,' the gunmen melted with horror and fear. Their guns went off they knew not how and they shrank down in their holes waiting for death.

48 Shangoedi's second charge did actually carry the breach so that the whole palace was at her mercy. But just then not only she and her warrior party, but Nagulo's men who were attacking on the other side, withdrew and were seen to be engaged in a violent dispute. No one in the palace could understand the reason of this marvellous deliverance, until one of the besiegers shouted over the wall that Mallam Ali had been captured and it was disputed whether to put him to death or no. At this Waziri, who had seemed in a dying state all night, suddenly revived and declared that he himself would fetch the police. Clerk Williams volunteered to join him, saying that he alone as the King's representative could authorize the police to take action.

Williams, a Gold Coast man, much valued by Bradgate for his efficiency and good sense, showed great courage and guile in this enterprise. It was he who saw that the besiegers' sudden diversion gave a good opportunity for escape, not by the back way but by the market place; and that the smoke of the burning houses sometimes blew across the front gate of the palace. He and Waziri slipped out under cover of this smoke and, though they were seen and fired at, they were safe among the compounds before anyone could catch them.

49 The barracks at Yanrin lie behind the Residency bungalow and consist of the usual lines of mud huts drawn up in ranks like men on parade. The guard room, a square flat-topped mud house shaped like a large brick, stands at one corner. It has a porch of corrugated iron on four crooked posts to shelter the guards and the clock, an American kitchen clock which lies on its back in a hole cut into the front wall of the house next the door. It will not go except on its back. A rail about a yard long is hung from the iron roof by a rope threaded through a bolt hole; this is the bell on which the hours are struck.

When Waziri and the clerk reached the barracks at a quarter to nine the cleared square about the huts and the guard room was enlivened by the whole official population of the barracks and most of their friends and servants, parasites equivalent to twice as many again, who were running about in great excitement. The wives could be seen assisting each other in cleaning the carbines; one woman grasped the rifle, the other with an expert movement drew out the pull-through, then carefully inspected the barrel; others were rolling the red cummerbands which a Nigerian policeman wears round his waist under his belt; little boys were proudly scrubbing their fathers' buttons, and the fathers themselves, some naked, some only in shorts, some in their shirt tails, were calling out to their wives, servants, and to each other enquiries and instructions.

Every face showed animation and a keen interest in the moment, the air was full of excited cries, everybody was busily occupied, so that Waziri at his first sight of them exclaimed with a great sigh of relief: 'At last—at last they're getting ready.' He rushed into the camp waving his long arms and shouting in a lamentable voice: 'Hurry—hurry—they are mur-

185

dering everybody. Do not wait longer. Come quickly with all your guns.'

Most were too busy to pay any attention to him; a few looked in surprise at the old man's torn clothes and wild antics. A barrack boy carrying a calabash of water paused to ask him: 'Is it true that Owule's village has been burnt?'

'Owule's village! Prophet of God! they've burnt Kolu, they've burnt Yanrin.'

'Straw is cheap,' said the boy laughing.

'Yes, and pagans,' another cried.

'So they're going to roast old Owule. They'll need to put some fat to him,' a woman said, in such a comical tone that the bystanders shouted with laughter.

Waziri threw up his hands in astonishment and ran on towards the guard room, which was surrounded by a thick crowd. Sergeant Moma Sokoto could be seen there seated on an ammunition box in the porch, in his usual corner between the clock and the rail. He was listening, but with an indifferent, expressionless face, to three women who were screaming their complaints. They had been amusing themselves at Fanta's in Kolu when the rioters attacked it and pulled them out. They had been robbed and beaten. One thrusting her swollen face close to the sergeant's shouted: 'See here, Sergy, see what they have done to me.'

The sergeant did not move. Someone in the crowd of women and barrack boys shouted: 'Sergy doesn't see any difference.'

At this all but the sergeant burst into a roar of laughter; even the injured woman burst out laughing. The crowd rained jokes.

'Why didn't you run away, Fatu? Did you want to see what they were going to do?'

'Did they do it, Fatu?'

'You only have to hit yourself in the other eye and you'll be as beautiful as a hippopotamus.'

186

Waziri and the clerk struggled to make their way through this laughing crowd, crying every moment: 'Make way, make way, it is the Waziri, it is the clerk.'

But no one minded them. In barracks they were persons of no importance, strangers in a foreign country with its own laws and interests and, moreover, a good deal of genial contempt for civilian aliens. It was not until a small boy, belonging to one of the constables and related to Waziri through his wife, recognized the visitors, that they were admitted. The small boy shouted angrily: 'Make way there—I want to see Sergy,' and way was made. Waziri, staggering with weariness, breathless with excitement and urgency, precipitated himself into the clear space before the sergeant and began at once to shout that the police must come at once. Yanrin was being destroyed. Alkali and Zeggi were murdered, his own son was in the hands of the enemy.

'And look at this,' Williams cried, showing his trousers torn, his hat broken, a cut on his nose. 'It is an outrage, I tell you. I am sending in a strong complaint to high quarters. Time is not to waste, Sergeant Moma. You should get the men with guns and sufficient ammunition and proceed at once to strong steps. That is my order.'

Sergeant Moma was a Fulani and strongly resembled Umaru and other pure bred men of his desert race in the extreme thinness of his ramshackle bony frame, his long, pale face and long nose. His mind was logical, his manners dignified, his self-control imperturbable, his self-respect, founded on his mastery of himself and his circumstances, not to be surpassed by any other Fulani or Arab in the country. He rose now to his height, about six foot, and without so much as glancing at Waziri or the clerk took up a heavy bar of wood and struck nine times on the rail. The blows singing from the iron and making the porch roof clatter like thunder drowned even the clerk's shrill voice.

The bugles sounded, the guard fell in, and loud agonized cries were heard from a young lady who had not yet oiled down her husband's legs: 'No, it is not nine irons—Sergy is wrong—only look at the sun down there.'

The clerk was shaking his hands in the air and yelling, 'It is an order, I tell you, an order.'

The sergeant gazed over his head into the distance.

The crowd were laughing at the clerk: Where are your pretty shoes, clerk? The sun has gone through your hat.

A Hausa lance corporal who had been rolling himself into his cummerbund by advancing slowly, turning all the way, towards a friend, now began to call for his carbine, and received it from a small naked daughter of eight or so who informed everybody with pride, 'I cleaned it myself.' This little piece of vanity made the crowd laugh again, and meanwhile the corporal, having examined his carbine, his legs, flicked a speck of dust from his blue shorts and pulled the creases at the side to make them stand out, had leisure to notice the clerk, and remarked to him in a kindly way: 'We can't shoot people like that, clerk. It's not allowed. Our orders are to guard the money.'

'But this is an order,' Williams shouted at him. 'An order, I tell you. If you do not immediately follow this order I will report you all to the judge. I will write to the King of England, I will write a letter to the newspaper. You will all be put in prison, I swear by God.'

Waziri, who had enough English to know that his mission was not enjoying immediate success, tore his beard and moaned. He swayed to and fro like an old horse about to fall.

The good-natured corporal spoke again, explaining things to these stupid laymen: 'Why, you see, clerk, Bradgy didn't give us any orders to do any fighting. He always tells us to stay in barracks and we're not allowed to go out with our guns at all. Why, when I was at Berua, the Sergy lost his stripes for stopping a row in the market. Some of the people there were murdering a Yoruba, and he called up a couple of his men and made them run. Well, what happened then? One of 'em that had a little tap over the head was brother to some clerk or other and the clerk sent a letter to the gumna (governor) and they took the Sergy's stripes away.'

This sad story received plenty of corroboration from the bystanders, who accompanied it with a continuous burden of: 'That's so, what a shame, I was there myself. They're always down on the Dan Sanda' (policemen).

'So you see,' the corporal ended, 'we can't go out with guns unless we have orders.'

'And we don't take them from anyone but Bradgy,' cried another policeman, bending over the guardroom cooler to see in the water the angle of his tall blue fez, which he carefully adjusted.

Waziri was incoherent. He grasped the corporal by the arm and gibbered at him: 'But you can't—they've caught Ali now.'

The corporal gently freed his arm and gave the old man a tap on the chest: 'Sorry, papa, but just think a moment. When Bradgy comes back he will count our cartridges. Now do you see.'

Waziri could not see. He threw himself on his knees before the Sergeant and beat his head on the ground, screeching for mercy as if he had committed a crime.

The sergeant, who had not betrayed the faintest interest either in the story of the Berua sergeant or the clerk's furious threats, now for the first time glanced at the old minister. His long face showed complete indifference to the fate of all these local savages, whether Christian or pagan, excitable negroes like Williams or noisy barbarians like Waziri, men without mastership, without quality.

He rose and made a slight gesture, the corporal roared:

'Fall in,' the crowd rushed aside. Good-natured persons seized Waziri and the clerk and dragged them backwards: 'Look out, you're in the way.'

The sergeant began carefully and methodically to inspect the guard, who underwent at the same time the critical examination of the whole barracks.

50 The Nupes had brought Ali to Yanrin during the night, and after two hours' haggling sold him to Brimah for ten shillings. But as soon as Shangoedi heard of this transaction she demanded the boy for herself.

Brimah, who expected to get twenty pounds reward for him, either from Waziri or his mother's family, would not give him up for nothing. A furious dispute broke out at once between his party, chiefly Hausa and Kolua, and Shangoedi's, who were largely Yerubas from the mission.

Both sides cursed and shouted at the top of their voices, and the audience which included Fanta and half the blackguards, male and female, of Kolu, most of them drunk, encouraged them with yells of laughter and jokes.

Suddenly Ojo rushed in with Makoto and Nagulo, who were dressed in new chief's gowns taken from some district head's town house. Ojo himself was wearing a white gown like a surplice, but it was too large for his stick-like limbs. The boy was wasted and trembling with fatigue, but the energy of excitement worked in him like an engine. His arms whirled, his bloodshot eyes darted here and there, the quivering lips poured out words, orders, angry cries, appeals, in a series of hoarse treble yells.

He was enraged with the disputants and flung himself among them shrieking: 'Drunkards, fornicators. What den, you spoil de Kingdom. God destroy you, you heathen men.'

190

Shangoedi flew at him in her rage, but Makoto, devoted to Ojo, took her up in his arms and carried her kicking away.

When the dispute was explained to Ojo he ordered that Ali should be produced. Ali was brought out. Brimah and the Kolua, especially Fanta's women, had treated him kindly, fed him, dressed his wounds with leaves, but he was a miserable object without his gown and sword. Like most boys of his age he was thin and gawky, his joints large, his shins crooked. His feet appeared enormous. His ugly frog-like countenance was rendered still more ugly by fatigue and terror.

Ojo having told him that God had decreed the end of all the devil's kingdoms, including Yanrin and England, and the destruction of all unbelievers, asked him if he would agree to become a Christian.

Ali made a sound in his throat but failed to answer.

A woman's voice suddenly called out: 'Leave him alone. He is a Christian.'

But Makoto shouted angrily that Ali was a Mahomedan, everybody knew that.

'He isn't. He follows Jesus.'

Ali licked his lips and said in a faint voice: 'Jesus, yes, I follow him.'

The Kolu people, who were mostly blackguards quite indifferent to religious questions, come to Yanrin for loot and free beer, set up a yell of triumph so that Ojo who was shouting something could not make himself heard. But Makoto, who had just got rid of Shangoedi to Nagulo, now came pushing back to the help of his leader, and roared at Ali: 'What, you follow Jesus, that's a lie.'

'No, no, it's true. Jesus, he's a good man. He's a prophet.'

The Kolua mob set up another yell, but Makoto roared them down and Ojo, quivering, spluttering in his rage with the fools, screamed at them: 'You don't understand—you don't understand. The Muslims call Jesus a prophet. It's in their religion. They have stolen him. But they do not worship him. They say he is not a god.' Catching Ali by the arms, he shook him and screamed at him: 'Don't lie now, you Mahomedan pig—is Jesus a god?'

Ali tried to answer, but he could not get his tongue to say yes. Even though he was blind with fear and unable to keep his trembling muscles still he could not confess himself publicly a coward. He was ashamed before the crowd. He opened his mouth to speak but nothing came from his throat, so that he looked like an imbecile, guilty, weak.

'You see,' Makoto yelled, 'he denies Jesus. He denies him. Fetch a whip.'

But just then one of Fanta's women called Hadesa, reckless on account of high spirits and drink and the encouragement of the Kolua men, flew between Ojo and Ali and screamed at the two Christian leaders.

'Off with you, it's none of your business. Can't you see he's only a fool of a boy.'

'Hold your tongue, punk.'

Makoto struck Hadesa a blow in the stomach that laid her screaming on the ground, but her Kolu friends immediately threw Ojo and Makoto out of the house.

Ojo was sobbing with humiliation and fury. 'Wait, wait,' he shrieked.

Hadesa, also weeping but with pain, screeched at him from the doorway in her prostitute's voice, hoarse and broken. 'Pox rot you, you white man's boy. You and your god are the same. Big heads that don't like to see other people happy.'

The blasphemy was received with yells of laughter and applause, and the quarrel growing always more violent went on for half an hour. Ojo cursed Brimah's people in the name of God and they laughed at him.

But Shangoedi, having won over Nagulo, returned with all

her women's and Nagulo's spearmen. They charged into the Alkali's house from all sides, cut Hadesa's and Brimah's throats, killed Fanta because as a beer-seller she had been denounced by Carr, and dragged out Ali by the legs. He was claimed at once by Shangoedi and the women.

Ali, knowing now that he was about to die, prepared himself to do the right thing and show the dignity and courage befitting a gentleman and a pupil of the Berua school.

He found this easier than he looked for. He had expected to be frightened, he forced himself to resist fear, but now in the crisis when Shangoedi, knife in hand, crouched over him, straddling his legs, grinning with joy, open-mouthed as if for a good meal, he had no leisure for fear. He was occupied entirely with the difficulties of keeping his self-control and dignity in this awkward position, before the eyes of the women crowded closely round, greedy and eager to see him flinch. He kept his eyes fixed on Shangoedi, closed his mouth (he knew that this was one of his ugliest features) and sought to look calm and haughty. In this he thought he was succeeding. He was pleased with himself. He felt honourable.

Shangoedi, reading his mind, grinned more broadly and said to her girls in a mournful voice: 'You see, he's not afraid,' and then to Ali, 'Oh you big man, too proud for Shangoedi, too proud to cry out.'

Ali at these words resolved to die rather than utter a sound, but Shangoedi was too much for him. He had expected death at a blow, or at least in a few minutes. But he was not allowed to lose consciousness for half an hour, and all his dignity was lost in the first minutes. Soon he was screaming, begging to be killed. But to the end he did not regret his bold enterprise. He had no time for leisure or regrets.

When at last he could not be revived the mob, intoxicated by the long draught of cruelty, tore his body to pieces and even broke up his bones as if to make them also suffer. Many put pieces of flesh into their neck-bags for charms or philtres. For Ali had been a mallam. He could read and write and therefore he had magical powers. They were still quarrelling over the division when a shout was heard: 'The police.' At once all led by Shangoedi herself fled from the place in every direction.

In fact the Berua detachment was still on the road and the Yanrin police in their barracks. This alarm which together with the disputes about Ali and his execution saved the court and three hundred refugees in Yanrin palace from massacre, was caused only by Sergeant Moma Sokoto who had come to town for his usual morning promenade.

As the Christians bolted his tall extremely thin figure with the fez over one eye and the swagger stick in the armpit was seen moving at a slow march towards the market place. It was a procession of one man.

51 The Christians made for Ketemfe, which is the nearest border town to Yanrin and a favourable place for escapers because it stands at the corner of three divisions, Yanrin, Berua and Daji. Besides, it is surrounded by thick bush and its people are not at all inclined to support any government. At least a hundred refugees including most of the leaders were gathered at Ketemfe before three o'clock waiting for the ferry. But meanwhile the Ketemfe natives, who at the first coming of Ojo's party had hidden their boats and fled into the bush, took courage, and when the ferries from Shibi were seen approaching they ran out into the shallow water and drove them off with spears.

The senior headman of the two villages, a man called Gani, then told Ojo and Makoto that none of their people would be allowed to leave Ketemfe until the rain had fallen.

It was no good for Ojo to point to the sky which was full of rain clouds and shout: 'Look at the rain, you fool.' Gani, with the shrewdness of a countryman answered calmly: 'Rain in the sky does not make the yams grow.'

Gani's people supported him with a fury that astonished Ojo and Makoto. But all the pagans had set their hopes on the Christians since Aissa's first success. Even now it is said in Yanrin that the Christians are the only reliable rain makers; better even than a Hausa.

'Make the rain or we'll kill you,' they shouted. 'You killed Owule. You've driven Oke away. No one but you is left to give us rain now. Make it quickly.'

Ojo continued to threaten and to implore. He pointed out that if Yerima came he would kill them all.

'Yes, but not us. He would praise us,' said Gani. 'If you do not set about making rain at once we will send for Yerima and you will all be broken or burnt.'

Some of Nagulo's men who tried to escape back across the neck of the peninsula were cut off there and speared to a man. Their heads and parts were tossed among those who stayed.

'See,' said Gani, 'you can't get away. We are too strong.' By this time in fact there were two thousand Kolua farmers gathered behind Ketemfe on the land side. Every man within ten miles who had spent the morning among his yam hills with his eyes fixed on the sky waiting for the promised tornado, had caught up his spear and run to Ketemfe at the news that the rain-makers were trying to escape without fulfilling their contract.

'Make us the rain and make it fall here, not in Shibi,' they bawled.

The late comers, who had run a long way through the bush, were in a worse temper and asked leave to kill some of the Christians at once. 'Kill the thieves, the liars, send them after

Owule. All these jujumen are liars and thieves.' Spears were thrown and a woman from Shibi was wounded. Ojo fell on his knees and began to pray. The others crowding close about him and Makoto uttered cries of despair.

Gani drove back his men with his staff of office surmounted by the royal crown and shouted: 'As soon as the rain falls, we will give you the boats. Even the first drops.'

The Christians promised that rain would fall within an hour. Ojo explained to God, as he had heard Mr. Carr explain and as far as possible in the same words, the needs of his people, and asked him to forgive them their sins, to take pity upon them in their extremity, and send a good rain.

All the Christians prayed, beating their heads on the ground. Those who did not know what Ojo was saying and knew no other formula repeated in English: 'Jesus loves me,' and added in their own tongue: 'Open the sky now.' Ojo's voice rose into a piercing cry: 'Hear us, God, hear us. We fear too much. We you people. You not fit to make us die. Oh God, you big strong God. It small ting for you to make rain fall. Oh God, you open your heart—you hear us—you our fadder and mudder.'

But already some of the people were shouting: 'Where's Aissa? She made the other rain. She's the only one that can save us.'

No one had seen Aissa since the night before, but many of the petitioners already doubting the value of their own prayers and anxious for a change of policy, jumped up at once and ran about calling for her.

Makoto and Ladije stole away from Ojo to direct the search; soon all but Ojo himself, and Old Sara and Kalé, who were kneeling with him, were hunting for Aissa. Angry cries were heard. 'She's run away from us—Gajere has taken her.'

The village was searched, then the jungle on each side.

Makoto's party going into the forest on the north heard shouts of laughter in a voice which was at once recognized as Aissa's. They broke through the thick undergrowth and found themselves on the edge of a deep narrow stream full of mud too soft and deep to cross. Owule's huts stood on the other bank of this creek, and it was from the nearest of them that the shrieks and guffaws could be heard, now louder than ever.

They shouted to Aissa by name, but she did not answer or cease laughing.

52 What had happened was this. Gajere having been imprisoned in Owule's village for the last month knew his way about and soon found beer and food with which he and Aissa celebrated a marriage feast. They were drunk all night, slept all morning, and having waked to the delight, still new and unexpected, of finding themselves together, they were now making love and getting drunk again. All the rest of Aissa's party, the Shibi women, had gone off to Yanrin with Ojo except a Fulani girl called Baju, one of Aissa's Bible class, whom she kept to wait on her.

Baju had two duties which she performed very well—to look after Abba and to watch outside the house. She had heard the first advance of Makoto's party and run in to give warning. But just at that moment Aissa and Gajere rolling about on the floor together knocked Abba against the wall and Baju, forgetting her mission, flew to save him. Aissa, swearing, had already snatched him away.

'See what you've done, you frog,' she shouted at Gajere, who opened his enormous mouth and uttered a drunken laugh. Aissa, having had the baby brought to her attention, poured out her feelings upon it: 'My dear, my darling, my little ape.'

197

She rocked it in her arms and offered it her breast. But it, slighted by this bribe instead of the reparation justly demanded by its injuries, sunk its head between its shoulders like a tortoise, curled its back, stiffened its arms, pulled down the corners of its mouth, and uttered a loud howl.

This made Aissa as well as Gajere shout with laughter. Baju, who had been bending over with a look of deep anxiety, also gave a joyful laugh and cried, 'The rascal.'

Aissa tossed it up and shouted, 'There we go.' These insults caused Abba to howl with rage. He knew very well that he was not going to get any compensation for his injustice, he was being cheated. But suddenly he forgot this huge grievance and smiled.

To Aissa and Gajere this seemed both pleasing and funny. They reeled about uttering peal after peal of laughter, weeping, clutching at each other. Gajere from his huge throat volleyed sounds like the heehaw of a jackass. Aissa moaned with the pain of this delightful time, hiccupped. They punched each other, swore at each other, rolled over like dogs at play, and as they did so forgot once more about Abba.

The Christians had stopped on the other side of the gully that ran beside the house; its undergrowth as well as the low walls hid Gajere and Aissa from them, but they heard them as plainly as if in the same room. Shouts rose: 'The beast, the murderer, catch them.' Makoto roared over and over again: 'Aissa, come, we want you.'

But when Baju, growing more frightened, managed to make Aissa understand that the mission people were calling for her she answered with amusement: 'Tell them to go away. I don't want them. I'm not going back any more.'

'No,' Gajere bellowed, 'she's not going back any more. She's coming with me.'

'I'm going with him.'

And both, thrusting their laughing faces out of the hole in the wall which served for a window on the gully side gazed with drunken grins at the angry Christians, and wagging their heads explained in a good-natured way that Aissa was done with the mission.

'What for I go back? I catch Abba now, I catch Gajere,' Aissa reasonably enquired.

'You go away, you let my woman alone, or I'll give you something.' Gajere, growing annoyed, began to threaten.

'I do plenty good for Jesus,' Aissa declared. 'Jesus, he do plenty for me. Good-bye now—all done finish,' and saluting her friends with some very rude gestures she broke into peals of laughter.

But just then Ladije's party, which, coming direct, had avoided the gully, began to tear down the fence on that side of the hut. Gajere and Aissa rushing out to escape found themselves in the midst of the crowd.

Gajere, yelling defiance at the top of his voice, poised his spear. He rushed at Ladije bellowing: 'You want Gajere. Here then.' But one of the women put a stick between his legs, and as he fell Ladije struck him with his matchet, cutting a great flap of skin and flesh from his head and laying bare the white bone of his skull. He fell stunned and the women would have finished him off at once with their knives and nails if Aissa, who had run back to push Baju and Abba into the undergrowth, had not come jumping and hopping back again in time to rescue him. She flew at the crowd like an angry hen, hooking her claws at them, shrieking curses. Even Ladije gave ground before her, confused and ashamed, uttering excuses. All were afraid of the witch.

She threw herself on her knees beside Gajere with howls like those of a dog lamenting its master and rolled him over, turned back the flesh that lay over his eyes. She breathed into his mouth, spat into his eyes, kneaded his stomach. Gajere began to twitch and roll his head. He tossed his arms and muttered: 'Come on, I'm Gajere. I am.'

Ojo came hurrying from the bush to see what was going forward. The boy was exhausted, his eyes filmed, his pallid chin streaked like a dirty window with sweat, his lips hanging open, marked by lines of dried foam. His emaciated head tottered on the long neck like a toy on a spring. He could scarcely hold himself upright on his trembling legs, and when he tried to kneel with Aissa he fell against her and supported himself by catching her by the arms.

He began at once to reproach the girl in a loud, shrill voice full of his grief and indignation: 'Sister, sister, what you do. You break ma heart now. What, you no fit turn God from us?'

Aissa was glad to see her friend. She was sure that she could make him understand her position and protested eagerly: 'No, no, Ojo, you don't hear proper, dese bad women beat Gajere ma man. I say what for dey beat ma man. Den dey curse me.'

The crowd, encouraged by the presence of their leader, were pressing forward again, and one young woman carrying a big two-year child and showing every mark of exhaustion and panic, suddenly began to scream: 'Burn her—burn the witch. Where's her Jesus now. Where's the rain. Are we to die here?'

At once a dozen yells went up: 'Yes, give us the rain, you dirt. Give us rain now. No more tricks.'

Aissa turned her head to scream a few curses at them in the middle of her eager explanation to Ojo: 'I do all ting for Jesus, Ojo. Jesus tell me kill Owule. I killum. I give him ma foot (holding out her stump). I burn ma arm too (holding up her arm). I do all ting for Jesus. Jesus say, "You good girl, Aissa. You love me proper." He give me Gajere, he give me Abba. I go home now All done finish.'

200

But Ojo answered in his sad, reproachful voice: 'Sister, you drunk, I smell you. You lie with dat pagan man. You run away from Jesus.'

As soon as Aissa heard this voice something moved inside her like a small animal waking from sleep and shaking itself, and she was filled with terror. For she perceived that the spirit had found her, that it was already within her lying in ambush. Immediately she heard it say in a very little quiet voice: 'Yes, Aissa, you bad.'

She broke from Ojo and sprang up intending to dash her head against a tree and throw out the spirit, but the women caught her. She leapt like a fish in their hands, and throwing back her head screamed at the sky: 'I not bad, Jesus. I good girl. I love you. I give you all ting. You lemme go now.'

But the spirit answered her at once without a moment's hesitation: 'Dat's lie, Aissa. You love Gajere more dan Jesus.'

'I no love dat Gajere,' she shrieked, and Gajere, stirred by his name, threw up arms and legs like a horse rolling and turned over on all fours. He began to drag himself towards Aissa, muttering, 'I'm all right, I am. Leave me alone, you'd better.' The crowd was shouting, 'Kill him, don't let him touch her.' The young woman with the baby thrashed him with a branch, shrieking abuse.

Aissa thrust her aside, knocking the branch from her hand but at the same time she furiously abused Gajere. 'You go way, you Gajere. You no good for nutting. You no ma man, I no lak you.' She spoke in English, although Gajere did not know a word of English. But she wanted Jesus to overhear.

Then seeing Ladije and some others closing in with their matchets and spears she grew more desperate. She snatched a knife from one of them and slashed herself across the chest, crying, 'I love you proper, Jesus. I cut myself for you. You help me now, I die for you.' She staggered to and fro, pushed Ladije backwards, nearly fell, recovered herself, and at last tumbled heavily, as if by accident, across Gajere, knocking him flat and lying upon him so that no one could strike him except through her body.

Then she contined to moan: 'See, Jesus, I love you, I die for you.'

But the spirit being inside Aissa, wrapped into every part of her being, knew her better than herself. It knew the wifely appetites of her body, the tingling love in her hands, the mother's desire of her full breasts, the greedy cunning of all her muscles, the deceit of her quick tongue and grimacing features, the pride, the vainglory of her obstinate heart, much sooner than her brain conceived a thought. It answered her therefore with much disgust: 'You fool girl, Aissa, you tink you cheat Jesus. You lie on Gajere, keep him safe. You love Gajere mo dan Jesus. You hit yourself with the back of the knife. Why you take care you no cut your breast, Aissa. You tell me dat? You keep you milk for Abba. You love Abba mo dan Jesus.'

When Aissa saw which way the spirit's mind was moving she was in such terror that she gave up the pretence of dying. She sprang up and seized her head in both hands as if to tear it off.

She saw Gajere raising himself from the ground and several of Ladije's boys running forward with spears to stab him; but she did not try to save him. She knew she must give him up. Nothing less could satisfy this spirit.

'You lie,' she shrieked; 'Gajere no ma man. I no lak Gajere at all. I you woman, Jesus. I give you all. I give you ma nose, I give you ma mouf. I no good for no man no mo.'

She drove the knife into her nostrils and mouth, splitting nose and cheeks; the people threw themselves on their knees

202

cutting and striking themselves in a frenzy and shouting: 'All for Jesus.'

The deep glade now filling with shadows as the sun turned over towards Berua was crowded with worshippers in every posture of appeal and devotion; their gabbled prayers, their moans of contrition, the loud piercing cries and sobs of mothers terrified for their children, and the children's wails of hunger, ascended for a considerable distance in the still hot air, and could be heard even in Ketemfe village, where it resembled the noise of sparrows frightened by a hunter or hawk.

Aissa had thrown herself down hoping that the spirit would think her dead. But the spirit said to her in a mournful voice: 'Ma poo girl, you poo sister Aissa, you say you give all ting you lak de most to Jesus. You tink you cheat him den.' Aissa sprang up again as if pricked by a spear. She knelt and looking up through the branches to the sky she held out her hands and said in a tone of surprise and incredulity: 'What, Jesus, you tink I lak anything better than dat man. What is it, you tell me den.' She parted her thick lips in an attempt to grin incredulously through the moustache and beard of blood which stiffened her muscles: 'What is it, den, I no lak nutting mo dan Gajere. What,' she raised her eyebrows and gaped in a laugh, 'You tink I lak dat bad pagan baby—dat boy no good for nutting, he silly bad chile—I doan care nutting for him.'

She called out to Baju: 'You catch dat bad Abba, Baju.'

Baju came out of her hiding place among the trees. Aissa took the baby from her back and put it into her arms, saying in English: 'Take him and throw him in de fire. He's no good. I no lak him no more.'

Baju, not understanding, took back the baby, which opened its eyes and recognizing its mother's voice and smell began to cry, holding out its arms stiffly like pegs and looking at her. It was too young to reach out its arms towards her;

203

it could only seek to embrace her, to draw her near, with its eyes.

'Ah, the nasty thing, take it away,' said Aissa in Hausa. Baju took the baby away. Aissa cried out indignantly to Jesus: 'What, you tink I lak dat nasty little ting. See I throw him into the river.'

Then she hopped after Baju and took the baby and put it under a bush. With trembling hands she took off its cloth and wrapped it round a stone which she held to her heart while she hurried to the river. She wept loudly: 'Oh Jesus, you right, I love him better, oh dear, ma poo lil baby. Oh I doan want to give him up. Oh baby, don cry no mo. You go to Heaven. Jesus make you happy for Heaven.'

Then she threw the stone into the river and flung herself down uttering loud howls: 'Oh my poo lil baby. Oh Jesus, I give you all. You go way now.'

The people came running up. Some of them supposed she had really thrown her baby into the river and their faces showed their gratification. It was felt that something important had been done at last.

Makoto in great excitement was shouting in the Kolua tongue: 'That's right. That's a good present. There's no better one to show a proper love. That pleases God.' The men smiling with joy shouted and jostled round Aissa to congratulate her, the women uttered those long prolonged screams which are the proper salutation for important chiefs.

Shangoedi and Sara began suddenly to sing in Yoruba the hymn, a favourite at the mission:

> 'When I look on the cross of wood
> On which they hung my Jesus.'

Men and women were deeply moved and sang with all their hearts. The hymn with its long notes drawn out by the men to the furthest possible extent and the wailing cries of the women rose among the tall trees like organ music and made the pagan watchers along the river tremble with fright.

The women had fallen on their knees, drawing Aissa down among them. Some in Yoruba, others in English, sang

> 'All de tings I lak de mos
> I sacrifice dem to His blood.'

Aissa could not sing. She moaned and put her hands over her ears to keep out the noise, she cursed the spirit, saying: 'I no care for you, I damn you. I no do nutting for you no mo. You go way now.'

But the music beat upon her, and already it was making her heart weak. Her strong badness was dissolving away.

She leapt to run away, uttering screams of rage and despair so piercing that the hymn singers were stayed with their mouths open and the watchers on the shore came running; but the women held her and Sara struck up the next verse.

Then Aissa fell on her face and cried: 'I shamed now, Jesus. Yes, I shamed. I repent. I too much sorry now. You forgive me.'

What a bad girl she had been. She was disgusted by her wickedness. She could not bear it. She struck her head on the ground and beat herself with her fists, crying: 'Oh! I bad, I bad. I too bad-hearted girl.' Sobbing loudly she confessed her selfishness, her drunkenness, her bad conduct with Gajere, her trick with the stone.

At first no one could understand what she was talking about, but Baju, who had been watching the proceedings with anxious attention, at last perceived what was in her mind and, glad to be helpful to her revered mistress, ran to fetch Abba from his hiding place.

Aissa did not even look at the child. She knelt between Sara and Shangoedi, who supported her, and sang with them

> 'All de tings I lak de mos.'

Her voice was interrupted by sobs and faint cries of joy. She was atonished by the peace, the happiness that had in one moment released her soul from the terror and agony of the long struggle. What had she been fighting for? What had she wanted, that fool girl Aissa, screaming like a child to keep the rubbish it has put into its mouth? Why had she for a second time forgotten what all the wise ones, the Carrs and Ojo and Sara had told her, that by doing the Lord's will, and not her own, she would be happy; by asking nothing for herself, she would be satisfied.

'I sacrifice dem to His blood.'

Tears of relief ran down her cheeks. What joy it was to give. She cried loudly: 'Take all, Jesus. I give you all, ma dear.'

This loud cry removed the last anxieties and doubts of the Christians, who broke into yells of excitement and triumph. Many began to dance; they laughed and struck at one another.

Makoto rushing from the wood carried a cross of two rough sticks tied together with a creeper. 'Stop, stop,' he bellowed; 'wait.'

He planted the cross in front of Aissa and looked round. 'Where's the baby?'

Abba was with Baju a few yards away. The girl was tickling him and laughing with him, while he, without paying any attention to her, was staring with amazement at his own fingers.

A dozen voices shouted: 'Hi, there, you. Don't you hear? It's wanted.'

Baju, ashamed of her levity, snatched up Abba and ran with him to Makoto, who began to instruct Aissa.

He pointed the child head first at the cross and said: 'Hold him this way, so that the blood will wet it.'

But now a furious dispute broke out. Nagulo, Shangoedi, Sara, Makoto all held different views and each had supporters even more positive and angry. Ojo too, roused from his private agony of appeal on the shore, where he still expected the boats from Shibi, came staggering back with hoarse cries of protest to which nobody paid much attention.

Others as well as Ojo objected to the sacrifice but on different grounds. Sara considered Abba not fit to be offered because he was blemished, and she quoted: 'Ye shall offer a male without blemish.'

Some wanted Aissa to be killed instead of Abba, because they held that God would be more pleased to see her killed after her recent bad conduct. Many who approved the sacrifice demanded that the cross should be put on a mound. Ladije continued to point out that he had himself often seen dogs sacrificed, but never without a mound.

But Makoto and Shangoedi by their loud voices and violent conviction bore down all the rest. They pointed out that they knew all about sacrifices. The cross did not need a mound, which was a pagan thing. Abba was a virgin boy and his hernia did not matter. It was not technically a blemish as it did not deprive him of any function. As for Ojo, who was still crying murder, a score of exasperated experts yelled at him that Aissa wanted to give Abba. It isn't murder, they shouted at him: 'She wants to do it, so the rain come.'

But he continued to curse and implore until they knocked him down and beat him senseless. Two women dragged him into the bush by the feet. His last cries were drowned by the hymn of sacrifice sung by a hundred voices. Makoto and Ladije once more set up the cross and began to clear a space round it.

But suddenly Ojo covered with blood started up among them like a jack in the box, screaming with a voice that overwhelmed every other sound.

'It is juju,' he shrieked. 'You fools, you make juju now to God, he damn you all, he blast you to hell, you damn pagans, you bloody damn pagan fools. You want go for hell den to de burning fire.'

Horror and rage at their blasphemy gave him the power and look of a demon. The miracle of his resurrection as if from the dead, his ghastly look in the evening light, mottled as he was with blood and dirt, his loud shrieks and violent gestures made even Makoto give ground. The hymn faltered into silence and the congregation hastily scrambled away before him, leaving him a clear path to Aissa. He plunged towards her with outstretched arms, pouring out triumphantly commands and reproaches. But she, not knowing what had happened or that she was singing by herself, continued to kneel in front of the small cross, her eyes closed, her whole body swaying to and fro while she cried in ecstasy

'All de tings I lak de mos
I sacrifice dem to His blood.'

Her joyful voice, her look of exaltation, the disfigurement of her face pierced Ojo to the soul. In that moment he perceived that she and Makoto were right and he was wrong. He had called them pagans because of their pagan rites—but their hearts were more Christian than his. He was fighting against the very spirit of love and sacrifice, against the wisdom of Jesus and the power of the Holy Ghost.

He fell on his knees before the woman and kissed her wounds. Astonished by the violence and suddenness of his conversion he wept and cried loudly:

'Glory, glory, glory, oh what joy, what glory to give all for Jesus.'

These shouts were echoed by the people who were at once reassured by the unexpected change of mind in their leader. They pressed round the pair in such a state of spiritual elation that they appeared to be mad drunk. Screams, catcalls, loud laughs almost drowned Makoto's powerful voice while he instructed Aissa. He had thrust Abba feet foremost into her arms, but she did not notice the child. She was singing in chorus with Ojo, who knelt beside her holding her waist. Her eyes were closed. Ojo's were turned upwards to heaven. His words came from him in cries and moans of adoration: 'Oh what joy, oh what joy to love him.'

Aissa echoed: 'Oh what joy, what joy.' She swayed on her knees, dancing with joy, smiling to herself.

The baby began to cry. It tried to grasp its mother's face or breast; but Makoto held it down by placing his hand on its back, and asked Aissa: 'Do you give it to Jesus?'

'Yes, yes, everything.'

Ladije instantly cut off the child's head with a blow of his sword. The blood spurted on the ground short of the cross. 'Hold it up,' Makoto shouted. Aissa let the body slide to the ground. Ladije snatched up the body and poured the blood on the branches.

'She must do it, she must do it,' Makoto shouted. 'That's no good.'

But Aissa, wedged between Ojo and Sara, continued to sing with closed eyes

'All de tings I lak de mos
I sacrifice dem to His blood.'

They could not make her understand what they wanted, and while they were shouting at her a messenger came running to tell them that some mounted men from Yanrin were at the village. The party scattered at once, all running about in confusion, the women looking for their children and their bundles, the men for some leader or group with which to join themselves. All were shouting questions, warnings, threats. They were ready to obey anybody or to murder anybody.

Some rushed at Ojo and shook their spears at him, shouting, 'You brought us here, now what shall we do?'

But Ojo did not even perceive them. He looked up to the sky, now growing dark, and cried: 'Oh de joy, de joy of de Lord.'

The larger number gathered round Makoto who knew what to do. Having prayed he took the cross and spun it on its short upper stem. All pressed close watching it. It fell with its shaft pointing towards the Ketemfe river.

The river had a deep mud bottom and in normal years was considered unfathomable. It was therefore not guarded by the pagans in force. Some of the Christians burst into indignant cries: 'That's no good—it doesn't mean that way.'

But Makoto shouting, 'Follow, follow, follow,' lifted the cross above his head and ran without hesitation into the water.

A watcher set by Gani cried a warning to him and then ran towards the village. Makoto went straight forward. The water rose to his chin, to his mouth, then sank to his neck. He was mounting the opposite bank.

With loud cries of joy and gratitude to God all ran down into the water and followed his course, the tall men holding up the shorter, the children on their mother's shoulders.

Yerima and his men reached the shore before the last fugitives had climbed out of the water, but they knew that it was useless and dangerous to follow into Daji country.

They caught therefore only Ojo and Aissa, who locked together were kneeling beside Abba's body, crying out: 'Oh de joy, oh de joy, de joy of de Lord.' They were weeping and laughing at the same time.

Even Ajala was afraid to go near them and the horses turned aside. But old Yerima, fearless in his religious zeal, spurred his horse up to them and cut Ojo down. Ajala's men broke the witch, but even while they struck her she continued to cry out louder than ever, 'Oh de joy, oh de joy.' The pagans having dragged her to the nearest ants' nest ran away as fast as they could.

53 Aissa, confused and drowsy, continued to whisper her love and gratitude to Jesus until she fell asleep. In the morning when the ants found her she tried to drag herself away from them. But she could only wriggle in a circle. She rolled on them, thrashed them with her forearms, crushing them by hundreds. But they were soldier ants born and bred for self-sacrifice. Probably also on account of the bad season they were especially eager to get food for their community; they were totally careless of wounds or death.

Their bites like fire obliged her to call out, her shrieks were heard for a long time by the Ketemfe people, but no one dared to go into the wood. Gani set a watch that nothing might come out.

Aissa soon grew weak; she could not remember where she was, the fire of the ants' tearing at her body did not scorch, it was like the warmth of flesh. Jesus had taken her, he was carrying her away in his arms, she was going to heaven at last to Abba and Gajere. Immediately the sky was rolled up like a door curtain and she saw before her the great hall of God with pillars of mud painted white and red. God, in a white riga and a new indigo turban, his hands heavy with thick silver rings, stood in the middle and beside him the spirit like a goat with white horns. Abba was sitting on its back looking frightened and almost ready to cry. One of the angels was holding him and putting his cap straight. The others were laughing at him and clapping their hands.

211

Aissa fearing that he would cry and disgrace himself with the important company waved and beckoned to attract his attention. At once as if feeling that she was there he looked down at her and smiled gravely.

Aissa held out her arms to him and shouted, 'Oh, you rascal.' She could not help laughing at him. She was helpless with laughter.